Paddington on Top

Paddington on Top

MICHAEL BOND

Illustrated by Peggy Fortnum

A YEARLING BOOK

Published by
Dell Publishing Co., Inc.
1 Dag Hammarskjold Plaza
New York, New York 10017

Yearling ® TM 913705, Dell Publishing Co., Inc.

ISBN: 0-440-46818-3

Reprinted by arrangement with Houghton Mifflin Company

Printed in the United States of America

Third Dell Printing—November 1979

Contents

1 Paddington Goes to School   7

2 Paddington Cleans Up   23

3 Paddington Goes to Court   39

4 A Birthday Treat   55

5 Keeping Fit   74

6 Paddington in Touch   89

7 Comings and Goings at
  Number Thirty-two   106

CHAPTER ONE

Paddington Goes to School

'Paddington has to go to school?" exclaimed Mrs Brown. She clutched at the front door of number thirty-two Windsor Gardens and gazed at the man standing on the step. "But there must be some mistake. Paddington isn't a . . ." She broke off as Mrs Bird gave her a nudge. "I mean he's a . . ."

"May I ask *why* he has to go to school?" interrupted the Browns' housekeeper.

The man consulted a pile of papers in his hand. "According to our information," he said, "he's been living here for a number of years and we've no record of a single attendance at St Luke's or anywhere else for that matter."

"But he was brought up in Darkest Peru," exclaimed Mrs Brown. "His Aunt Lucy taught him all she knew before he left. She had to go into a Home for Retired Bears in Lima, you see, and . . ." Her voice trailed away as she caught sight of the expression on the School Inspector's face.

"I'm very much afraid," he said, allowing himself a slight smile, "that neither the Home for Retired Bears in Lima nor Aunt Lucy happen to be on our list of approved establishments."

He snapped the file shut with an air of finality. "We shall expect to see him at school first thing tomorrow morning," he continued sternly, "otherwise certain steps will have to be taken."

Mrs Brown gazed after the Inspector as he disappeared down the road. "Tomorrow morning!" she repeated. "What *are* we going to do?"

"I think," said Mrs Bird wisely, "there's only one thing we *can* do. Make sure that bear arrives on time. After all," she added meaningly, "we do have his circumstances to think of. I daresay it's only a matter of the authorities setting their records to rights, but until they do I think we'd better tread very carefully.

"And if Paddington *is* going to school tomorrow," she continued, "we'd better get busy as well. I must sew a name-tag on his duffle coat for a start. We shall never hear the last of it if that gets lost." Mrs Bird paused at the kitchen door. "Will you tell him or shall I?"

Mrs Brown gave a sigh. "I will," she said.

She knew exactly what Mrs Bird meant. Ever since Paddington first arrived on the scene she'd had a nagging fear in the back of her mind that something like this would happen if only because they'd never actually reported his arrival to anyone, and the thought of breaking the news to him was not one she exactly relished.

But Paddington took the matter surprisingly well, and while the others busied themselves getting his things ready he spent the afternoon going through some of Jonathan and Judy's old text books. The rest of the time he spent polishing his suitcase, and that evening he even had a bath without being asked, which was most unusual.

All in all, he looked so spick and span the following morning even Mrs Bird's eagle eyes were unable to find fault.

"I still can't believe it," said Mrs Brown, as he set off down the road. "The house'll seem so quiet without him."

Mrs Bird gave a snort. "I should make the most of it," she said. You mark my words, it'll be four o'clock and he'll be back home again before we've had time to turn round."

All the same, it was noticeable that the Browns' housekeeper spent an unusually long time cleaning the step that morning, and she didn't finish it until long after the small figure in a duffle coat and hat had disappeared round the corner.

But Paddington himself didn't have any time to dwell on the matter. The school was only a short distance away from Windsor Gardens and as he drew near one of the teachers hurried forward to greet him.

"Good-morning," he said. "I take it you're one Brown, P?"

"One *brown pea?*" repeated Paddington in surprise. He gave the man a hard stare. "No, I'm not. I'm Paddington Brown."

The man let go of Paddington's paw. "Er . . . that's really what I was asking," he said nervously. "I have instructions to check your arrival. If you hurry you'll just be in time for the roll."

Paddington licked his lips. A roll sounded a very good way in which to start the day. "I think I shall enjoy that," he announced.

"Good," said the man, looking somewhat relieved. "We thought we'd put you in the Lower Fourth to start with. Mr Eustace's class. That's until we've had time to check your capabilities." He beckoned to a boy who was standing nearby. "Smith Minor will show you where to go."

"Gosh! Fancy putting you into old Eustace's class," said the boy sympathetically, as he led the way into the main building. "Hard luck! I should watch it. If he gets his knife into you you'll be for it."

Paddington looked around nervously as he followed the boy into the classroom. It was a large room, with windows running the length of one side. There was a blackboard

on an adjoining wall and a number of desks were dotted around facing it. But although there were several other pieces of equipment he couldn't see any actual cutlery, and he breathed a sigh of relief as he was ushered towards the front of the class.

There were about thirty other pupils already in the room and they all crowded round, anxious to make his acquaintance. Paddington was a popular figure in the neighbourhood and most of the class wanted him to sit near them.

There was soon an argument raging, and it was while the excitement was at its height that the door suddenly opened and an angular figure in a tweed suit entered the room.

"What's the meaning of this?" he bellowed. "Back to your desks at once!"

Standing on a platform in front of the blackboard he glowered down at the class as they scurried to their places.

"Now," he called sarcastically, when order had been restored, "I assume I have your permission to take the roll?"

Anxious to make a good impression on his first day, Paddington busied himself behind his desk lid. "I shan't be a moment, Mr Eustace," he called. "I've nearly finished. I've got over thirty-three already!"

"Over thirty-three?" repeated the form-master in surprise.

"That's right," said Paddington. "That's one each and three spare."

"*One each and three spare?*" Mr Eustace stared at Paddington as if he'd suddenly lost the use of his hearing. "Three spare *what?*"

"Marmalade sandwiches," explained Paddington cheerfully. He lowered his desk lid. "I hope they'll do. I'm afraid I didn't bring any rolls. But I've got some sliced loaf and some of my special marmalade from the cut-price grocers."

"*Marmalade sandwiches!*" spluttered Mr Eustace. He bounded from the platform, all thoughts of checking the list of those present driven from his mind as he peered inside Paddington's desk.

"I've a good mind to take these to the headmaster!" he cried.

It was Paddington's turn to look as if he could hardly

believe his ears. "All thirty-three?" he exclaimed in amazement. "Even *I've* never managed that many."

"Silence!" shouted Mr Eustace as a titter ran round the room.

"I mean," he said, breathing heavily as he turned back to Paddington, "that I am confiscating them. Marmalade sandwiches indeed! I've never heard of such a thing."

Paddington slumped back into his seat. He'd never heard of anyone having their marmalade sandwiches confiscated either, and he looked most offended.

"You're not here to learn how to make sandwiches," said the master as he removed the pile and placed it on his own desk. "You're here to learn the three R's."

"The three R's?" repeated Paddington in surprise. Despite his feeling of indignation at the unexpected loss of his sandwiches, he couldn't help being interested at this sudden turn of events. "I didn't know there were *three* R's."

"Ah," said Mr Eustace, with satisfaction. "We learn something new every day. The three R's," he continued, "are Reading, Writing and Arithmetic, and today we happen to be starting with arithmetic."

He turned to the blackboard. "Now," he said, pointing to some figures, "I have written out a little problem, and I've made a deliberate mistake. Can anyone tell me what it is?"

In his haste to be first with the answer Paddington nearly fell off his seat. "I can!" he exclaimed, raising his paw as high as he could.

"Ah, Brown," said the master, eyeing him slightly less disapprovingly. "I'm glad to see you're quick off the mark. What is your answer?"

"You don't spell arithmetic with an R, Mr Eustace," said Paddington excitedly.

Mr Eustace stared at him. "I know you don't spell it with an R," he said impatiently.

Paddington's jaw dropped. "But you just said you did," he cried hotly. "You said there were three R's. Reading, Writing and Arithmetic."

"You did, sir," chorused the rest of the class.

Mr Eustace passed a trembling hand over his forehead. It suddenly seemed unusually warm in the classroom. "I may have *said* it," he began, "but I didn't mean it. That is ... I ..."

"I remember what it looks like," continued Paddington, pressing home his point. "My Aunt Lucy taught me, and she used to write it down. It begins with an A."

"I'm afraid," said the master wearily, "that I'm not familiar with your Aunt Lucy's curriculum."

Paddington opened his suitcase. "I'll show you a picture of her if you like, Mr Eustace," he announced. "Then you'll be able to recognise it. She had it taken just before she went into the Home for Retired Bears . . ."

"I mean," said Mr Eustace testily, "that I don't know anything about her teaching capabilities – *if* she has any."

Paddington gave him a hard stare. It was one of his hardest ever. He was a polite bear at heart, but he was beginning to get upset by the way the conversation was going, especially when it had to do with his Aunt Lucy.

"She's very good at spelling, Mr Eustace," he said stoutly. "She's always sending me postcards . . ."

"Are you suggesting, bear," thundered Mr Eustace, "that I am not?"

"Oh, no, Mr Eustace," said Paddington earnestly. "I'm sure it's very good to get one out of three right."

Mr Eustace mopped his brow again as another titter ran round the room. He was normally very keen on discipline, but for some reason or other he seemed to be losing his touch on this particular morning. It was definitely one of those days. For a moment or two he appeared to be taking advantage of his own arithmetic lesson by practising some counting, and then, as his eye alighted on the pile of marmalade sandwiches, a thought seemed to strike him.

"Since," he said, "you clearly have an interest in food, you may like to go out and do some shopping for me."

"Oh, yes, please," said Paddington eagerly. He felt as keen as Mr Eustace to bring the present topic of conversation to an end. "I often do Mrs Bird's shopping for her."

"Good," said Mr Eustace. "Perhaps we've found our true vocation at last."

Paddington's face fell. "Are you coming too, Mr Eustace?" he asked.

"No," said Mr Eustace, slowly and distinctly. "I shall not be coming too. But it so happens I need some fish . . ."

"Some fish?" echoed Paddington, nearly falling over backwards with astonishment. If Mr Eustace had asked for some chalk for the blackboard or even some rolls, he wouldn't have been surprised; but fish was the last thing he'd expected.

"Fish," repeated Mr Eustace, handing him some money. "Something in the nature of a herring or two would do admirably. You may," he added hopefully, "take as long as you like."

"Bears are good at shopping," said Paddington as he took the money and hurried towards the door, watched by thirty envious pairs of eyes. "I shan't be long."

Mr Eustace gazed after the retreating figure as if that was exactly what he feared, and sure enough, he'd hardly had time to bring the mathematics lesson to an end when the door burst open and Paddington hurried back into the room clutching a parcel wrapped in newspaper.

He looked rather apprehensive as he made his way towards the platform. Mr Eustace was clutching a knife in one hand and he appeared to be doing something to the contents of an old tin can.

"That was quick, bear," he said, trying to make the best of things as he looked up. "We're about to get under way with the next lesson."

Placing the knife on the table, Mr Eustace took the parcel and started to unwrap it. As he did so the smile slowly disappeared from his face. Normally fairly red, his features began to resemble an over-ripe beetroot as he undid the last of the folds.

"And what is this, pray?" he demanded, holding a package up to the light.

"It's some fish fingers, Mr Eustace," said Paddington. "They were a special offer in the supermarket. The man said they would be all right so long as you eat them before next Tuesday."

"*Eat them!*" Mr Eustace glared at the package. "I don't want to *eat* them. I want to cut them up! They're for my biology lesson."

Reaching over, he grasped the knife on his desk and with one sweeping movement pushed the tin can towards Paddington.

"Take this, bear," he thundered. "I shall call on you when it's time for practicals."

Paddington needed no second bidding. He had no idea what Mr Eustace had in mind, but from the look on his face and the way he was brandishing the knife, he had no wish to stay and find out. Clutching the tin in his right paw he backed towards the classroom door. When he

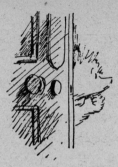

reached it he held his other paw up as high as it would
go.

"If you please, Mr Eustace," he exclaimed, "I think I
would like to be excused." And without waiting for an
answer he disappeared up the corridor as fast as his legs
would carry him.

Paddington was the sort of bear who believed in going
right to the top in times of trouble, and this definitely
seemed to be one of those occasions.

On his way in that morning he'd noticed a door marked
'Headmaster' and he didn't stop until he reached it.

The headmaster looked up in surprise as Paddington
entered his study and collapsed into a chair in front of his
desk. "I think Mr Eustace is going to put his knife into
me!" he gasped. "He wants to call on me for his practicals!"

St Luke's was a large school, and like all large schools
it had its fair share of problems. Even so, the headmaster
began to look more and more unhappy as he listened to
Paddington's tale of woe. He hadn't been best pleased
when the Inspector had passed on the news of a new
arrival halfway through the term, especially one who

apparently hadn't been to school before, and it seemed as though his worst fears were being realised.

He stood up as a bell began to ring somewhere in the distance. "It does seem as though it's been one long misunderstanding," he said. "That's the mid-day bell. Perhaps we can talk about it over lunch. There's nothing like a spot of food for calming the nerves."

Ushering Paddington through the door, he led the way down the corridor. "You may eat at the masters' table," he continued. "Just for today I'll make you food monitor. That means you'll be in charge of all the serving."

Paddington began to look more cheerful as he listened to the headmaster's words, and when he saw the pile of food laid out ready for them he grew more cheerful still, despite the fact that out of the corner of his eye he could see Mr Eustace glaring at him from the other end of the table.

After he'd finished serving out the soup Paddington turned his attention to an enormous tureen full of stew.

"I think I shall like school after all," he announced, licking his lips as he passed the first plateful to the headmaster.

"I'm very pleased to hear it," said the head. "After all," he added, "you'll be with us until you're sixteen, and that's a long time."

"Sixteen!" The ladle fell unheeded from Paddington's paw, and his eyes nearly popped out of their sockets as he gazed at the headmaster. "*Sixteen!* but I thought I was only here for the day!"

19

The headmaster gave a nervous chuckle. "I'm afraid it's the law now," he said, hurriedly turning to one of his colleagues. "And there's no getting away from it."

Paddington served the rest of the food as if in a dream. In fact he was so taken up with his thoughts that he quite forgot to give himself any, and several of the masters were already passing their plates up for seconds.

When he came to again, Paddington began peering into the pot with a thoughtful expression on his face.

"Come along, bear," called Mr Eustace impatiently. "Don't let it get cold. There's nothing worse than cold stew."

The headmaster looked round. "Is anything the matter?" he asked. "You look as if you've lost something."

Paddington poked the contents of the pot with a spoon.

"I think I may have dropped Mr Eustace's tin in the stew by mistake," he announced.

All eyes turned towards the end of the table as a loud groan followed Paddington's remark.

The headmaster jumped to his feet in alarm. "Are you all right, Mr Eustace?" he asked. "You seem to have gone quite pale."

Looking at Mr Eustace even his best friends would have had to admit that the headmaster's remarks about his complexion were the understatement of the year. He looked positively green as he sat clutching his stomach. "That tin," he moaned, "happens to belong to my biology class. It's the one I keep my worms in!"

Paddington looked up from the stewpot. "Would anyone else like any seconds?" he asked hopefully.

The headmaster removed an invisible speck of dust from his lapel as he gathered his thoughts. It had taken him a long while to explain to the Browns all that had happened to Paddington at St Luke's. It hadn't been an easy task, particularly as he still wasn't sure of all the facts himself.

"The long and short of it is," he said, "we . . . er . . . that is, my colleagues and I, feel that until young Mr Brown has a proper school uniform he'd be much better off staying at home."

"A school uniform?" broke in Mrs Brown. She looked at Paddington. "But we shall never get one to fit him."

The headmaster gave a cough as he rose to his feet. "Er . . . exactly," he said. "I've had a word with the Inspector and in the circumstances he's perfectly happy to take my advice. All in all I think it will be much the best thing."

He paused at the door and looked back at Paddington with the suspicion of a twinkle in his eye. "I'm sure you'll be pleased to know," he said, "that your suspicions were ill-founded. Mr Eustace's tin hadn't fallen in the stew after all. We found it under the table. Both the worms and Mr Eustace are doing very well.

"I have a feeling," he said, addressing Mrs Brown as he made to leave, "that in any case there's not much we at St Luke's can teach bears."

"I wonder what he meant by that last remark?" said

Mrs Brown, when she came into the room after saying goodbye to the headmaster. "Have you any idea, Paddington?"

But Paddington had his eyes closed. One way and another it had been a tiring day at school and he wasn't at all sorry to put his paws up.

Mrs Brown sighed. She sometimes wished it wasn't quite so hard to tell what he was thinking.

"If you ask me," said Mrs Bird, reading her thoughts, "it's probably just as well. There's no knowing what we might find out — especially when it comes to school-bears!"

CHAPTER TWO

Paddington Cleans Up

Paddington peered through the letter-box at number thirty-two Windsor Gardens with a look of surprise on his face.

In point of fact he'd been watching out for the postman, but instead of the blue-grey uniform he'd hoped to see, Mr Curry, the Browns' next-door neighbour had loomed into view. Mr Curry looked as if he was in a bad temper. He was never at his best in the morning, but even through the half-open flap it was plain to see he was in an even worse mood than usual. He was shaking a rug over the pavement, and from the cloud of dust surrounding him it looked as though he had been cleaning out his grate and had just had a nasty accident with the ashes.

The expression on his face boded ill for anyone who happened to come within his range of vision, and it was unfortunate that his gaze alighted on the Browns' front door at the very moment when Paddington opened the letter box.

"Bear!" he bellowed. "How dare you spy on me like that. I've a very good mind to report you!"

Paddington let go of the flap as if it had been resting in hot coals, and gazed at the closed door with a very disappointed air indeed. Apart from an occasional catalogue he didn't get many letters, but all the same he always looked forward to seeing the postman arrive, and he felt most aggrieved at being deprived of his morning's treat, especially as he'd been half-expecting a postcard from his Aunt Lucy in Peru. Something she'd said when she'd last written had given him food for thought and he was anxiously awaiting the next instalment.

All the same, he knew better than to get on the wrong side of Mr Curry, so he decided to forget the matter and pay his daily visit to the nearby market in the Portobello Road instead.

A few minutes later, having taken his shopping basket on wheels from the cupboard under the stairs, he collected Mrs Bird's shopping list, made sure the coast was clear, and set out on his journey.

Over the years Paddington's basket on wheels had

become a familiar sight in the market, and it was often much admired by passers-by. Paddington took great care of it. He'd several times varnished the basketwork, and the wheels were kept so well oiled there was never a squeak. Earlier in the year Mr Brown had bought him two new tyres, so all in all it still looked as good as new.

After he'd completed Mrs Bird's shopping, Paddington called in at the bakers for his morning supply of buns. Then he carried on down the Portobello Road in order to visit the antique shop belonging to his friend, Mr Gruber.

Paddington liked visiting Mr Gruber. Apart from selling antiques, Mr Gruber possessed a large number of books, and although no one knew if he'd actually read them all, it certainly seemed as though he must have, for he was a mine of information on almost every subject one could think of.

When he arrived he found Mr Gruber sitting on the horsehair sofa just inside his shop clutching a particularly large volume.

"You'll never guess what today's book is about, Mr Brown," he said, holding it up for Paddington to see. "It's called 'Diseases of the Cocoa Bean', and there are over seven hundred and fifty pages."

Paddington's face grew longer and longer as he listened to Mr Gruber recite from the long list of things that could happen to a cocoa bean before it actually reached the shops. He always rounded off his morning excursions with a visit to his friend, and Mr Gruber's contribution to the meeting was a never-ending supply of cocoa, which he kept at the ready on a small stove at the back of the shop. It didn't seem possible that this could ever come to an end.

"Perhaps we'd better get some more stocks in, Mr Gruber," he exclaimed anxiously, when there was a gap in the conversation.

Mr Gruber smiled. "I don't think there's any risk of our going short yet awhile, Mr Brown," he replied, as he busied himself at the stove. "But I think it does go to show how we tend to take things for granted. We very rarely get something for nothing in this world."

Paddington looked slightly relieved at Mr Gruber's reassuring words. All the same, it was noticeable that he sipped his cocoa even more slowly than usual, and when

he'd finished he carefully wiped round his mug with the
remains of a bun in order to make sure he wasn't letting
any go to waste.

Even after he'd said goodbye to Mr Gruber he still had
a very thoughtful expression on his face. In fact, his mind
was so far away it wasn't until he rounded a corner leading
into Windsor Gardens that he suddenly came back to
earth with a bump as he realised that while he'd been in
the shop someone had pinned a note to his shopping
basket.

It was short and to the point. It said:

YOUR SHOPPING BASKET ON WHEELS IS IN
SUCH GOOD CONDITION IT SHOWS YOU HAVE
CHARACTER, DRIVE AND AMBITION. THIS MEANS
YOU ARE JUST THE KIND OF PERSON WE ARE
LOOKING FOR. YOU COULD EARN £100 PER WEEK
WITH NO MORE EFFORT THAN IT TAKES TO VISIT
THE GROCERS. I WILL BE IN TOUCH SOON WITH
FURTHER DETAILS.

It was written in large capital letters and it was signed
YOURS TRULY. A WELL - WISHER.

Paddington read the note several times. He could
hardly believe his eyes. Only a moment before he'd been
racking his brains to think up ways of earning some extra
money so that he could buy Mr Gruber a tin or two of
cocoa; and now, out of nowhere, came this strange offer.
It couldn't have happened at a better moment, especially

as he'd been tempted to break into the savings which he kept in the secret compartment of his suitcase, and which he held in reserve for important occasions, like birthdays and Christmas.

It was hard to believe he could earn so much money simply because he'd kept his shopping basket clean, but before he had a chance to consider the matter he saw a man in a fawn raincoat approaching. The man was carrying a large cardboard box which seemed to contain something heavy, for as he drew near he rested it on Paddington's basket while he paused in order to mop his brow.

He looked Paddington up and down for a moment and then held out his hand. "Just as I thought!" he exclaimed. "It's nice when you have a picture of someone in your mind and they turn out exactly as you expected. I'm glad you got my note. If you don't mind me saying so, sir, you should go far."

Paddington held out his paw in return. "Thank you, Mr Wisher," he replied. "But I don't think I shall go very far this morning. I'm on my way home." He gave the man a hard stare. Although he was much too polite to say so, he couldn't really return the man's compliments. From the tone of the letter he'd expected someone rather superior, whereas his new acquaintance looked more than a trifle seedy.

Catching sight of Paddington's glance, the man hastily pulled his coat sleeves down over his cuffs. "I must apologise for my appearance," he said. "But I've got rid of . . . er, I've obtained so many new clients for my vacuum cleaners this morning I don't know whether I'm coming or going. I haven't even had time to go home and change."

"Your *vacuum cleaners!*" exclaimed Paddington in surprise.

The man nodded. "I must say, sir," he continued, "it's your lucky day. It just so happens that you've caught me with my very last one. Until I take delivery of a new batch later on, of course," he added hastily.

Taking a quick glance over his shoulder, he produced a piece of pasteboard, which he held up in front of Paddington's eyes for a fleeting moment before returning it to an inside pocket.

"My card," he announced. "Just to show that all's above board and Sir Garnet like."

"You, too, could become a member of our happy band and make yourself a fortune. Every new member gets, free of charge, our latest model cleaner, *and* . . . for today only, a list of do's and don'ts for making your very first sale.

"Now," he slapped the box to emphasise his point, "I'm not asking twenty pounds for this very rare privilege. I'm not asking fifteen. I'm not even asking ten. To you, because I like the look of your face, and because I think you're just the sort of bear we are looking for, *two* pounds!"

His voice took on a confidential tone. "If I was to tell you the names of some of the people I've sold cleaners to you probably wouldn't believe me. But I won't bore you with details like that. You're probably asking yourself what you have to do in order to earn all this money, right? Well, I'll tell you."

"You sell this cleaner for four pounds, right? You then buy two more cleaners for two pounds each and sell *them* for four, making twelve pounds in all, right? Then you either keep the money or you buy six more cleaners and sell those. If you work hard you'll make a fortune so fast you won't even have time to get to the bank."

"Another thing you may be asking yourself," he continued, before Paddington had time to say anything, "is why anyone who already has a vacuum cleaner should buy one of ours?"

He gave the box another slap. "Never fear, it's all in here. Ask no questions, tell no lies. With our new cleaner you can suck up anything. Dirt, muck, ashes, soot . . . pile it all on, anything you like. A flick of the switch and whoosh, it'll disappear in a flash."

"But," he warned, "you'll have to hurry. I've a queue of customers waiting round the next corner."

Paddington needed no second bidding. It wasn't every day such an offer came his way, and he felt sure he would be able to buy an awful lot of cocoa for twelve pounds. Hurrying behind a nearby car he bent down and opened his suitcase.

"Thank you very much," said the man, as Paddington counted out two crisp one pound notes. "Sorry I can't stop, guv, but work calls . . ."

Paddington had been about to enquire where he could

pick up his next lot of cleaners, but before he had a chance to open his mouth the man had disappeared.

For a moment he didn't know what to do. He felt very tempted to take the cleaner straight indoors in order to test it in his bedroom, but he wasn't at all sure Mrs Bird would approve. In any case, number thirty-two Windsor Gardens was always kept so spotlessly clean there didn't seem much point.

And then, as he reached the end of the road, the matter was suddenly decided for him. Mr Curry's front door shot open and the Browns' neighbour emerged once again carrying a dustpan and brush.

He glared at Paddington. "Are you still spying on me, bear?" he growled. "I've told you about it once before this morning."

"Oh, no, Mr Curry," said Paddington hastily. "I'm not spying on anyone. I've got a job. I'm selling a special new cleaner."

Mr Curry looked at Paddington uncertainly. "Is this true, bear?" he demanded.

"Oh, yes," said Paddington. "It gets rid of anything. I can give you a free demonstration if you like."

A sly gleam entered Mr Curry's eyes. "As a matter of fact," he said, "it does so happen that I'm having a spot of bother this morning. I'm not saying I'll buy anything mind, but if you care to clear up the mess I *might* consider it."

Paddington consulted the handwritten list of instructions which was pinned to the box. He could see that Mr

Curry was going to come under the heading of CUSTOMERS
— VERY DIFFICULT.

"I think," he announced, as the Browns' neighbour
helped him up the step with his basket on wheels, "you're
going to need what we call the 'full treatment'."

Mr Curry gave a snort. "It had better be good, bear,"
he said. "Otherwise I shall hold you personally responsible."

He led the way into his dining-room and pointed to a
large pile of black stuff in the grate. "I've had a bad fall of
soot this morning. Probably to do with the noise that goes
on next door," he added meaningly.

"My cleaner's very good with soot, Mr Curry," said
Paddington eagerly. "Mr Wisher mentioned it specially."

"Good," said Mr Curry. "I'll just go and finish
emptying my dustpan and then I'll be back to keep an eye
on things."

As the Browns' neighbour disappeared from view
Paddington hurriedly set to work. Remembering the
advice he'd been given a short while before, he decided to
make certain he gave Mr Curry a very good demonstration indeed.

Grabbing hold of a broom which was standing nearby,
he quickly brushed the soot into a large pile in the middle
of the hearth. Then he poked the broom up the chimney
and waved it around several times. His hopes were
speedily realised. There was a rushing sound and a
moment later an even bigger load of soot landed at his
feet. Ignoring the black clouds which were beginning to

fill the room, Paddington removed the cardboard box
from his basket, and examined Mrs Bird's shopping. As
he'd feared, some of it had suffered rather badly under the
weight and he added the remains of some broken custard
tarts, several squashed tomatoes, and a number of cracked
eggs to the pile.

It was while he was stirring it all up with the handle of
the broom that Mr Curry came back into the room. For a
moment he stood as if transfixed.

"Bear!" he bellowed. "Bear! What on earth do you
think you're doing?"

Paddington stood up and gazed at his handiwork. Now
that he was viewing it from a distance he had to admit it
was rather worse than he had intended.

"It's all part of my demonstration, Mr Curry," he
explained, with more confidence than he felt.

"Now," he said, putting on his best salesman's voice as he consulted the instructions again, "I'm sure you will agree that no ordinary cleaner would be any good with this mess."

For once in his life it seemed that Mr Curry was in complete and utter accord with Paddington. "Have you taken leave of your senses, bear?" he spluttered.

Paddington gave the cardboard box a slap. "No, Mr Curry," he exclaimed. "Never fear, it's all in here. Ask no questions, I'll tell no lies."

Mr Curry looked as if there were a good many questions he was only too eager to ask, but instead he pointed a trembling finger at the box.

"Never fear, it's all in here!" he bellowed. "It had better all be in there! If it's not all in there within thirty seconds I shall . . . I shall . . ."

Mr Curry paused for breath, suddenly at a loss for words.

Taking advantage of the moment, Paddington opened the lid of the box and withdrew a long piece of wire with a plug on the end.

He peered at the skirting board. "Can you tell me where your socket is, Mr Curry?" he enquired.

If Paddington had asked the Browns' neighbour for the loan of a million pounds he couldn't have had a more unfavourable reaction. Mr Curry's face, which had been growing redder and redder with rage, suddenly went a deep shade of purple as he gazed at the object in Paddington's paw.

"My socket?" he roared. "*My socket?*" I haven't any sockets, bear! I don't even have any electricity. I use gas!"

Paddington's jaw dropped, and the plug slipped from his paw and fell unheeded to the floor as he gazed at the Browns' neighbour. If Mr Curry's face had gone a deep shade of purple, Paddington's — or the little that could be seen of it beneath his fur — was as white as a sheet.

He wasn't sure what happened next. He remembered Mr Curry picking up the cardboard box as if he was about to hurl it through the window, but he didn't wait to see any more. He dashed out through the front door and back into number thirty-two Windsor Gardens as if his very life depended on it.

To his surprise the door was already open, but it wasn't until he cannoned into Mr Gruber that he discovered the reason why. His friend was deep in conversation with the other members of the family.

For some reason they seemed even more pleased to see him than he was to see them.

"There you are!" exclaimed Mrs Bird.

"Thank goodness," said Mrs Brown thankfully.

"Are you all right?" chorused Jonathan and Judy.

"I think so," gasped Paddington, peering over his shoulder as he hastily closed the door behind him.

"No one's tried to sell you a vacuum cleaner?" asked Mrs Bird.

Paddington stared at the Browns' housekeeper in amazement. It really was uncanny the way Mrs Bird 'knew' about things.

"There have been some 'goings-on' down at the market this morning, Mr Brown," broke in Mr Gruber. "That's why I popped in. Someone's been selling dud vacuum cleaners and when I heard you'd been seen talking to him I began to get worried."

"When you were so late back we thought something might have happened to you," said Mrs Brown.

"Well," said Paddington vaguely, "I think it has!"

Paddington launched into his explanations. It was a bit difficult, partly because he wasn't too sure how to put some of it into words, but also because there was a good deal of noise going on outside. Shouts and bangs, and the sound of a loud argument, followed a moment or so later by the roar of a car drawing away.

"Fancy trying to take advantage of someone like that," said Mrs Bird grimly, when Paddington had finished.

"He seemed quite a nice man, Mrs Bird," said Paddington.

"I didn't mean the vacuum cleaner salesman," said

36

Mrs Bird. "At least he gave you *something* for your money – even if it didn't work. I meant Mr Curry. He's always after something for nothing."

"He's too mean to get his chimney swept for a start," said Judy.

"And I bet he's still waiting to see if electricity catches on before he changes over," agreed Jonathan.

They broke off as the telephone started to ring and Mrs Bird hurried across the hall to answer it.

"Yes," she said after a moment. "Really? Yes, of course. Well, we'll do our best," she added after a while, "but it may not be for some time. Probably later on this morning."

The others grew more and more mystified as they listened to their end of the conversation.

"What on earth was all that about?" asked Mrs Brown, as her housekeeper replaced the receiver.

"It seems," said Mrs Bird gravely, "that the police think they may have caught the man who's been selling the dud vacuum cleaners. They want someone to go down and identify him."

"Oh, dear," said Mrs Brown. "I don't really like the idea of Paddington being involved in things like that."

"Who said anything about Paddington?" asked Mrs Bird innocently. "Anyway, I suggest we all have a nice hot drink before we do anything else. There's no point in rushing things."

The others exchanged glances as they followed Mrs Bird into the kitchen. She could be very infuriating at times. But the Browns' housekeeper refused to be drawn, and it wasn't until they were all settled round the kitchen table with their second lot of elevenses that she brought the matter up again.

"It seems," she mused, "that the man they arrested was caught right outside our house. He was carrying a cleaner at the time. He said his name was Murray, or Hurry or something like that . . . Anyway, he insists we know him."

"Crumbs!" exclaimed Jonathan as light began to dawn. "Don't say they picked on Mr Curry by mistake!"

"I bet that's what all the row was about just now," said Judy. "I bet he was coming round here to complain!"

"Which is why," said Mrs Bird, when all the excitement had died down, "I really think it might be better if Paddington doesn't go down to the Police station. It might be rubbing salt into the wound."

"I quite agree," said Mr Gruber. "In fact while you're gone perhaps young Mr Brown and I can go next door and clear up some of the mess."

"Bags we help too," said Jonathan and Judy eagerly.

All eyes turned to Paddington, who was savouring his drink with even more relish than usual. What with Mr Gruber's book on diseases and the disastrous events in Mr Curry's house he'd almost begun to wonder if he would ever have any elevenses again.

"I think," he announced, as he clasped the mug firmly between his paws, "I shall never take my cocoa for granted again!"

CHAPTER THREE

Paddington Goes to Court

Mr Gruber was still laughing over Paddington's adventure with the vacuum cleaner when they met next morning.

"Fancy all that coming about just because I happened to be reading a book on cocoa beans, Mr Brown," he said.

He gave another chuckle. "I wish I'd seen Mr Curry being marched off to the Police Station. It must have been a sight for sore eyes."

Paddington nodded his agreement. His own eyes were

feeling sore at that moment, but mostly through keeping them tightly shut in case he bumped into Mr Curry.

Apart from his eyes, his paws were also rather stiff. It had taken them quite a while to clear up the mess in Mr Curry's dining-room, but many hands make light work, and it was generally agreed that not even the Browns' neighbour could have complained about the way his room looked after they had finished.

"Anyway," said Mr Gruber, as he brought out the tray for their elevenses, "all's well that ends well. Although I must say it's a good job it didn't happen in some countries I could think of. In some countries, Mr Brown, you are thought to be guilty until you are proved innocent, whereas here it's the other way round. It's a very fine point, but it can make a great deal of difference sometimes."

Paddington listened carefully while Mr Gruber went on to explain about the workings of the Law.

"It sounds very interesting, Mr Gruber," he said at last. "But it's a bit hard to understand if you've never been inside a court."

Mr Gruber slapped his knee. "Why didn't I think of it before?" he exclaimed. "If you could spare the time, Mr Brown, perhaps we could have one of our excursions. It's about time we had another outing. We could visit the Law Courts and then you could see what goes on. Would you like that?"

"Ooh, yes please, Mr Gruber," said Paddington eagerly. "I would like that very much indeed."

Paddington polished off the rest of his elevenses with all possible speed and then hurried back home to tell the others.

While he made some marmalade sandwiches, Mrs Bird prepared a flask of hot cocoa, and shortly afterwards he donned his duffle coat again and disappeared back up the road carrying his suitcase.

"I do hope they'll be all right," said Mrs Brown. "It's not that I don't trust Mr Gruber, but things do happen to Paddington and you know what some of these judges are like. I would hate to think of them both ending up in gaol."

"Knowing that bear," said Mrs Bird darkly, "I think it's much more likely that any judge he meets will end up giving himself six months!"

Paddington would have been most offended had he been able to overhear Mrs Bird's last remark, but by then he was already heading towards the bus stop where he'd arranged to meet Mr Gruber.

Paddington liked bus journeys, especially when he was able to sit on the top deck and listen to his friend talking. Mr Gruber knew a great deal about London, and if Paddington had any complaint at all it was that he always made the journey pass twice as quickly, so that it seemed no time at all before they drew up outside a group of imposing grey stone buildings and Mr Gruber announced that they had reached their destination.

He led the way through some tall iron gates and then up a flight of stone steps.

Paddington's eyes grew larger and larger as they passed through the entrance and he found himself in an enormous hall, almost as large as a cathedral. It was full of people bustling to and fro: some in ordinary clothes, others dressed in wigs and black gowns, and it was quite unlike anything he'd ever seen before.

Mr Gruber consulted his guide-book. "This is the main hall of the Royal Courts of Justice," he explained. "It's two hundred and thirty-eight feet long and eighty feet high."

He led the way up some more steps and suddenly they found themselves in a maze of corridors. "The courts themselves," he went on, "are dotted around the outside of the main hall, and you'll find that each one is hearing a different case.

"There are two sides to every disagreement, Mr Brown," he continued. "It's the job of the lawyers to argue the rights and wrongs and find out who is telling the truth."

"Can't they just ask them?" suggested Paddington.

Mr Gruber chuckled. "Unfortunately," he said, "the truth isn't always quite as simple as it looks, and even more unfortunately people aren't always as truthful as they like to make out. In the end it's the judge who has to make up his mind. That's why he's so important. It's like watching a television play – except, of course, it's much more serious if you happen to be playing one of the leading roles."

"Justice," said Mr Gruber, as he paused outside a door,

"not only has to be done, but it has to be seen to be done as well. That's why they have a Public Gallery, and it's the right of every citizen to be present if he so wishes."

Mr Gruber's face fell as he tried the handle. "Oh dear," he said. "It seems to be locked. How very disappointing. I'm sure there must be some mistake. If you care to wait here a moment I'll see if I can find someone in authority."

Excusing himself, Mr Gruber hurried off down the corridor leaving Paddington to wait outside the door. In point of fact he wasn't at all sorry to have a moment's rest so that he could take in all that Mr Gruber had told him, and there was so much activity all around he was only too happy to sit back and watch for a while.

Opening his suitcase, he took out a marmalade sandwich and then poured himself a cup of cocoa to while away the time. Mrs Bird's Thermos flask was a very good one indeed. It always kept things extremely hot, and the present contents were no exception. In fact, so much steam rose from the cup of cocoa he had to wipe his eyes several times in order to see what was going on.

He put the top back on the flask and had only just finished closing his suitcase again when a man in uniform came up to him.

He stared at Paddington in surprise. "What do you think you're doing?" he asked. "This isn't a snack bar you know."

"I'm waiting to go in," said Paddington. "I want to see justice done."

The man gave him an odd look. "What's your name?" he enquired.

"Brown," said Paddington. "Paddington Brown."

"Brown?" echoed the man. A change suddenly came over him. "Dear, oh dear," he said. "It's a good thing for you I came along. They're calling for you downstairs!"

"They're calling for me downstairs?" exclaimed Paddington. "Mr Gruber must have been quick!"

"I don't know about Mr Gruber," said the man, helping him to his feet, "but if you take my advice you'll get a move on."

Paddington needed no second bidding. Grabbing hold of his suitcase he hurried down a flight of steps after the man and rounded a corner into another long corridor where, sure enough, he heard someone calling his name.

"Here he is," called his companion. "Found him upstairs having a tuck in."

"Well, you'd better look slippy," cried the second man, waving him on. "It's old Justice Eagle today and he doesn't like to be kept waiting."

Looking most alarmed, Paddington hurried through some doors and suddenly found himself in a room full of people.

The whole of one half was taken up by rows of seats on tiers, not unlike a small theatre, and facing them behind a bench on a raised platform was an imposing looking man wearing a large wig.

He glared at Paddington over the top of his glasses. "Where have you been?" he asked severely. "I suppose you realise you've been keeping the court waiting?"

Paddington raised his hat politely. "I'm very sorry, Mr Eagle," he announced, "but I'm afraid my eyes got steamed up."

"Your eyes got steamed up?" repeated the judge. "Upon my soul! In all my years I've never heard of that one before!"

"Mr Gruber and I were trying to get in," said Paddington, "but we were locked out."

"You were locked out!" exclaimed the judge. He gazed round the court in the hope of seeing who might be responsible. "This is an outrage. I will not have people prevented from appearing in this way."

"Mr Gruber wasn't very pleased either," agreed Paddington. "He's gone to see if he can find someone in authority."

"Er . . . quite so," said the judge, looking slightly

more benevolent. He motioned to a man sitting in the well of the court. "Let us proceed. We've lost enough time already."

To Paddington's surprise the man led him to a box-like compartment at the side of the court and opened a small door for him.

Feeling very pleased that he was being given a seat with such a good view of all that was going on, Paddington climbed inside and was about to settle down when the man handed him a book.

"Do you swear?" he began.

"Never," said Paddington firmly. "Mrs Bird wouldn't like that at all. And even if she did I wouldn't."

The man looked around apprehensively at the judge and then decided to have another go. "Do you swear," he repeated, "to tell the truth, the whole truth, and nothing but the truth?"

"Oh, yes," said Paddington more cheerfully. "I was brought up by my Aunt Lucy, and she taught me never to tell lies."

"Silence in Court!" exclaimed the judge, as a titter ran round the assembly.

He consulted a sheaf of papers in front of him and then directed his gaze at a man in a wig and gown on the other side of the room.

"I see no mention of Aunt Lucy, Mr Cloudsworthy," he said. "Do I take it that the prosecution are not going to call her?"

"I don't think she would hear if you did, Mr Eagle," said Paddington. "She's in Peru."

"Aunt Lucy's in Peru?" repeated the judge. He adjusted his glasses and gazed at the prosecuting counsel. "I find this very hard to accept."

Mr Cloudsworthy looked as if he found Aunt Lucy's absence even harder to accept than the judge. Looking most confused, he shuffled through his own pile of papers and then had a hurried conversation with one of his assistants.

"Er, with respect, me lud," he said. "I don't think she's very important."

Paddington gave Mr Cloudsworthy a hard stare. "Aunt Lucy's not important!" he exclaimed. "She brought me up!"

"I think," said the judge, after a long pause, "that perhaps you'd better start your questioning, Mr Cloudsworthy. We will deal with the matter of Aunt Lucy later."

"Yes, me lud," said Mr Cloudsworthy. He turned and directed his attention towards Paddington. "I take it," he said, "that you realise why you are here today?"

"Oh, yes," said Paddington. "I'm here because it's my right as a citizen."

Mr Cloudsworthy looked slightly taken aback. "Er, yes," he said. "Very commendable. Very commendable indeed. I take it, from your reply, that you have some knowledge of the law. May I ask if you've ever taken articles?"

"Never!" exclaimed Paddington hotly. "That's worse than telling lies."

"I didn't mean those sort of articles," said Mr Cloudsworthy crossly. "I mean the sort you have to take when you learn a profession. It's like an agreement to say you have to stay with someone until . . ." He broke off under Paddington's steady gaze and hurriedly changed the subject.

"I'll have you know," he continued, "that I have a very big case here."

Paddington peered at him with interest. "I've got a small one," he announced, holding up his suitcase. "I brought it with me all the way from Darkest Peru. It's got a secret compartment where I keep all my important papers."

"Really?" said Mr Cloudsworthy, trying to strike a jocular note as he caught sight of the expression on the judge's face, "I thought perhaps that was where you kept your briefs."

"My *briefs?*" echoed Paddington. "I'm only here for the day."

The judge took hold of his gavel and rapped the desk sharply. "Silence!" he bellowed. "This is no laughing matter."

"Briefs," he said, turning to Paddington, "are papers lawyers have to bring with them when they attend court."

"Oh, I don't have any of those," said Paddington, opening his case. "But I've got some marmalade sandwiches."

"May I see that?" asked the judge, as Paddington held one of them up for everyone to see.

Paddington handed the sandwich to one of the ushers, who in turn crossed and passed it up to the judge.

"Is this really part of the evidence you are submitting, Mr Cloudsworthy?" demanded the judge distastefully, as he took a closer look. "A bear's sandwich!"

Mr Cloudsworthy looked as if he was hardly sure of anything any more. Removing a handkerchief from inside his gown, he lifted up his wig and began mopping his brow. "Er . . . I . . . er, I'm not really sure, me lud," he stuttered.

"Mark this sandwich 'Exhibit A'," said the judge, handing it back to an official. "I will examine it more closely later."

"My sandwich is being marked 'Exhibit A'!" exclaimed Paddington excitedly. "That's some of Mrs Bird's special home-made marmalade. She will be pleased."

"We'd better call her then," said the judge. "Perhaps she'll be able to throw some more light on the matter."

"I've never even heard of Mrs Bird!" cried Mr Cloudsworthy.

The judge looked at him severely. "I really don't think, Mr Cloudsworthy," he said, "that you are conducting your case in the best possible fashion. You don't even appear to know your own witnesses. Call Mrs Bird!"

"Call Mrs Bird!" shouted someone at the back of the court.

"Call Mrs Bird!" echoed a voice outside.

"I don't think she's here either, Mr Eagle," said Paddington.

"Mrs Bird's not here?" repeated the judge. "But she's obviously a most important witness. Why isn't she here?"

"I expect she's out shopping with Mrs Brown," said Paddington. "She always goes out Tuesday afternoons."

"Really!" barked the judge. "This is intolerable." He glared across the courtroom at the unfortunate defence counsel. "I've a very good mind to call a halt to the whole case."

Mr Cloudsworthy took a deep breath. "With the greatest respect, me lud," he said, "I would like to ask the witness one more question."

"Granted," said Mr Justice Eagle reluctantly. "But please do be brief."

Placing two trembling thumbs beneath his lapels, Mr Cloudsworthy fixed Paddington with his gaze as he made one last despairing effort.

"Where were you on the morning of the twenty-ninth?" he asked slowly and distinctly. "Think carefully before you answer."

Paddington did as he was told and considered the matter for a moment or two. "What time on the morning of the twenty-ninth, Mr Cloudsworthy?" he asked.

"At around eleven o'clock," said the defence counsel, looking slightly relieved that he was making some progress at last.

"I expect," said Paddington, "I was having my elevenses with Mr Gruber. We always have them round about then. That's why we call them elevenses."

"Call Mr Gruber," said the judge wearily.

"Call Mr Gruber," said a voice at the back of the court.

"Call Mr Gruber," came an answering echo from outside.

By that time everyone had become so used to the non-appearance of witnesses that a buzz of excitement went round the court as the door suddenly opened. Mr Gruber was accompanied by another man, and he looked more than pleased when he saw Paddington standing in the witness box.

"If you please, my lord," he said, addressing the judge. "I fear there has been a slight misunderstanding. As I'm sure your Lordship realises there are a good many Browns in this world, and I have a feeling that two of them have become mixed up." He motioned to the man standing next to him. "I believe this is the Mr Brown you really wanted to see!"

The judge first gazed at Mr Gruber and then at Paddington, rather as if he not only agreed that there were a good many Browns in the world, but that there was even one too many for his liking. He appeared to be about to say something and then changed his mind and rose to his feet.

"It's been a very trying day," he said, wearily. "I think I shall hear the rest of this case in my private chambers!"

Paddington and Mr Gruber paused at the entrance to the Law Courts and gazed back at the great hall, still seething with life.

"What a good thing I heard my name being called when I did," said Mr Gruber, "otherwise there's no knowing what might have happened. It only goes to show how very careful you have to be in these matters, and that even a judge should never take things for granted."

Paddington looked as if he couldn't agree more. "Fancy Mr Eagle liking marmalade sandwiches," he said. "He told me he wished he could have some in his chambers every day."

"Judges are only human," said Mr Gruber. "They may look very grand when they're in court, but take away their wig and robes and they're just like anyone else. Except, of course, they need to be much wiser than most people. And often much more understanding."

"I don't suppose there are many bears who can say they've been inside a judge's private chambers," he continued, "let alone shared their sandwiches with one."

It had taken Mr Gruber some while to explain matters to the judge but in the end even Mr Cloudsworthy had taken the matter in good part.

"Mr Cloudsworthy said that he wouldn't mind having

me as a witness on his side another time," said Paddington. "Especially if my eyes were steamed up. I wonder what he meant by that?"

Mr Gruber coughed. "We shall probably never know, Mr Brown," he said tactfully, "but if you want my verdict, after all the goings on we've been through I think we ought to have a nice cup of tea. There's a restaurant near here where they used to serve some delicious crumpets. If you still have any room left it might be worth investigating. What do you think?"

Paddington licked his lips. "I think, Mr Gruber," he said, as they made their way down the steps and into the world outside, "that you would make a very good judge too if you ever decided to be one."

CHAPTER FOUR

A Birthday Treat

Paddington pressed his nose against the door of the Brightsea Imperial Theatre and peered at a notice pinned to a board on the other side of the glass.

"I think we're in time, Mr Brown!" he exclaimed excitedly. "It's called 'Bingo Tonight', and it's on for two weeks."

Mr Brown joined Paddington at the door and looked in at the darkened interior of the foyer. "That's not a play," he said. "It's a game."

"You know," said Jonathan. "All the sixes, clickety-click."

"All the sixes, clickety-click!" repeated Paddington. He had no idea what the others were talking about, but he didn't like the sound of it at all.

"It means they've closed the theatre down," exclaimed Judy. "It's been turned into a Bingo Hall."

The Browns gazed at each other in dismay. It was Paddington's summer birthday, and as a treat they had decided to take him to see a show. The day had dawned bright and sunny and on the spur of the moment they'd set off to visit Brightsea, a large town on the south coast, where plays were often tried out before being put on in London.

Paddington had talked of nothing else all the way down, and the news that he was to be done out of his treat was, to say the least, a bad start to the day.

"Perhaps you'd like to go and see the gnomes in Sunny Cove Gardens instead?" suggested Mrs Brown hopefully. "I did hear they've all been repainted this year . . ." Her voice trailed away as she caught sight of the expression on Paddington's face. Even the brightest of gnomes was hardly a substitute for a visit to the theatre, especially when it was a birthday treat.

"We could go down to the beach while we think about it," said Judy.

Mr Brown hesitated. "All right," he replied. "We'll get some ice-creams on the way to be going on with."

Paddington brightened considerably at Mr Brown's remarks, and after casting one more glance at the deserted theatre he turned and followed the others as they made

their way along the road leading to the promenade.

Although he was disappointed about the play, Paddington wasn't the sort of bear to stay down in the dumps
for long, and when they came to a halt alongside a van
and Mr Brown ordered six ice-creams, including "a
special large cone for a young bear who's just suffered a
disappointment", he felt even better.

Clutching the ice-cream in one paw and his suitcase in
the other Paddington followed the rest of the family as
they trooped onto the beach. His suitcase was full of
birthday cards, a good many of which he hadn't really had
time to read properly, and he didn't want to let them out of
his sight before he'd been able to go through them all
again.

Mr Brown put some deck chairs near the water's edge,
and while Jonathan and Judy changed into their costumes
Paddington made some holes in the wet sand with his

57

paws and then let the incoming waves smooth them over again. It was all very pleasant, for the sea was warm, and calm enough to paddle in without getting the rest of his fur soggy.

It was while he was in the middle of making a particularly deep hole that he happened to glance up hopefully in order to see if there were any more waves on the way, and as he did so he suddenly caught sight of a speedboat. His eyes nearly popped out of their sockets as it shot past. In fact, if his paws hadn't been firmly embedded in the sand he might well have fallen over backwards with surprise.

It wasn't the boat itself that caused his astonishment, for the sea was alive with craft of all shapes and sizes: it was the fact that just behind it there was a man skimming along the surface of the water on what seemed to be two large planks of wood. But before he had a chance to take it all in, both boat and man had disappeared from view behind the pier.

Paddington sat down on the beach in order to consider the matter. It looked just like the kind of thing for a birthday treat, and he wished he knew more about it. But Mr Brown had settled down behind his newspaper for a pre-lunch nap, and Jonathan and Judy were having a swimming race and had already gone too far to ask. For a moment or two he toyed with the idea of mentioning his idea to Mrs Brown, but she was busy helping Mrs Bird with a knitting problem. In any case, he had a feeling in the back of his mind that she might not entirely approve, so in the end he decided he would have to do his own investigations.

Mrs Brown eyed him nervously as he stood up and announced his intention of taking a stroll along the promenade.

"Don't be too long," she warned. "We'll be having lunch soon. And I should take your duffle coat. It looks rather stormy."

Mrs Bird nodded her agreement. Since they'd arrived in Brightsea a change had come over the weather, and the sky was now more than half-covered by clouds, some of which looked very dark indeed.

"You'd better have my umbrella as well," she said. "You don't want to be taken unawares."

Mrs Bird followed Paddington's progress up the beach. She was never very happy when he went off on his own, especially when he was wearing one of his far-away looks.

"Perhaps he wants to stretch his paws after the long car journey," said Mrs Brown, with more conviction than she actually felt.

The Browns' housekeeper gave a snort. "He's much more likely to be looking for the ice-cream van again," she remarked.

All the same, Mrs Bird looked noticeably relieved when she turned and saw him peering at a row of posters on the promenade.

On the way down to the beach Paddington had spotted quite a number of advertisements, and although he hadn't actually read any of them he felt sure there must be at least one which would provide an answer to his question.

As he made his way along the front he stopped and examined several of them very carefully, but as far as he could make out, all they dealt with were things like Band Concerts and Mystery Coach Tours: none of them so much as mentioned boats let alone where he could buy any planks of wood.

Paddington had often noticed that whenever he went to the seaside all the really good events were due to happen the following week, and it wasn't until he was well past the pier that he suddenly came across the one he had been looking for.

It showed a man standing on the crest of a wave behind a large red speedboat. With one hand he was hanging on to the stern of the boat, and with the other he was pointing to a sign which said QUEUE HERE FOR SIGNOR ALBERTO'S INTERNATIONAL SCHOOL OF WATER SKI-ING.

There was some more writing underneath, most of which had to do with a special Crash Course for beginners, in which not only did Signor Alberto guarantee to get any of his pupils, regardless of age, out of the water and onto their skis in only one lesson, but he promised to present them with a special certificate afterwards to show their friends.

It all sounded very good value indeed, and Paddington was about to go down on the beach to where Signor Alberto's boat was moored, when he caught sight of yet another notice hanging from a nearby post. It said, quite simply: GONE TO LUNCH — BACK SOON.

Feeling somewhat disappointed, Paddington turned to retrace his steps. As he did so he saw some figures waiting on a bench a little way along the promenade. The bench seemed to belong to the ski-ing school as well, for as one of the occupants shifted his position he caught a brief glimpse of Signor Alberto's name chiselled into the wooden backrest.

In his advertisement Signor Alberto had said that he catered for anyone, no matter what their age, but as far as Paddington could make out some of his clients looked as if they would be hard put to make it to the boat, let alone climb inside. As he hurried along the front to join them he began to get more and more excited. He felt sure that if they were able to water-ski he would have no trouble at all.

"May I join you?" he enquired, raising his hat politely. The nearest man gave him an odd look. "I don't suppose it'll do any harm," he said grudgingly.

"The more the merrier," agreed the one sitting next to him as he shifted up to make room. "It'll help keep us all warm."

Paddington thanked them both very much and then squeezed in at the end. He waited for a moment or two, but no one else spoke. Indeed one man at the other end of the bench looked as if he was in great danger of falling asleep at any moment.

"Do you come here often?" he asked loudly, in the hope of livening things up a bit.

The man next to him nodded. "I've been here every day for the last six years," he said. "Come rain or shine. Mind you," he added, "you 'as to wrap up a bit on days like today."

"Wouldn't do to catch a chill," agreed his friend.

"You mean I can keep my duffle coat on?" exclaimed Paddington.

"Bless you, yes," said the first man encouragingly. "It's a free world. You do as you like."

Paddington settled back again with a pleased expression on his face. He'd been wondering what he could do with his belongings.

"Does it take you very long to get up?" he asked.

The man gave him another funny look. "About ten minutes," he replied. "But once I'm up, I'm up. Mind you, that includes shaving."

"Shaving!" exclaimed Paddington, nearly falling off the bench with surprise. He looked at his acquaintance with new respect. He'd been most impressed by the picture on the poster of the man hanging on to a rope with only one hand, but shaving at the same time was quite a different matter.

"I hope we don't have long to wait!" he exclaimed excitedly.

"I've been here since nine o'clock this morning," said a third man gloomily. "I got here at nine o'clock and I've been here ever since."

Paddington's face fell. Four hours sounded a very long time to wait for a ski-ing lesson, and he was just trying to make up his mind whether to go back and tell the Browns where he was and risk losing his place, or stay on for a little while longer in the hope that the queue would begin to move, when he felt a dig in the ribs.

"Watch out!" warned his neighbour. "Here comes the man in charge."

Paddington stared at the approaching figure. From the drawing on the poster he'd expected Signor Alberto to be large and bronzed, whereas the person coming along the promenade seemed quite the reverse. In fact, he was rather like a walking advertisement for indigestion tablets, and from the look on his face as he caught sight of Paddington it seemed as though he was just about to have another bad attack of his complaint.

As he drew near he held out his hand. "Right," he said grumpily. "Where's your book?"

"My *book?*" repeated Paddington. "But I haven't got one."

"Hah!" said the man triumphantly. "I thought as much. I daresay that explains why you're here. You probably can't read either."

Paddington gave him a hard stare. "I do a lot of reading!" he exclaimed hotly. "I always read a story under the blankets at night before I go to sleep. Mr Brown gave me a torch specially."

"I'm sorry," said the man sarcastically, "but we don't provide blankets here. I shall have to ask you to move on. Unless," he added, "you're over sixty-five?"

"Over *sixty-five?*" Paddington stared at the man as if he could hardly believe his ears. Although he had two birthdays a year he felt sure his latest one hadn't caused him to look that much older.

Already several passers-by had stopped to watch the proceedings and some of them started to join in.

"Fancy wanting blankets," said one. "Don't know what it'll come to next."

"Mollycoddling, I calls it," agreed another.

"Let him be," called a woman somewhere near the back. "We've all got to go that way sooner or later."

"Shame!" shouted someone else.

"That's all very well," said the man. "But I 'as my job to do. Suppose I let every Tom, Dick and Harry sit here, what then?"

"Tom, Dick and Harry?" repeated Paddington. He looked most upset. "I'm not one of those, Signor Alberto. I'm a Paddington."

"You're a Paddington?" echoed the man. Scratching

his head, he turned to the crowd for sympathy. "What *is* he on about?" he asked.

The man who'd been sitting next to Paddington rose to his feet as light began to dawn. "I think I know," he said.

He pointed to a notice on the back of the bench and then turned back to Paddington. "This isn't a queue for Signor Alberto," he explained. "This is a special bench for *Senior Citizens*. This gentleman's Alf, the deck chair attendant."

"Alf, the deck chair attendant!" exclaimed Paddington, as if in a dream. He gazed at the newcomer indignantly. "Do you mean to say I've been waiting all this time for nothing?"

"Not for nothing," said the attendant taking a ticket machine triumphantly from his inside pocket. "For ten pence. If you can't produce your old-age pension book on demand you 'as to pay ten pence an hour or else."

But he might just as well have saved his breath. Out of the corner of his eye Paddington had seen some activity around the ski-boat, and taking advantage of the argument, he stuffed Mrs Bird's umbrella inside his duffle coat and crawled through a gap in the crowd while the going was good.

He felt sure that if ever there was a time to take to the water this was it, and, hurrying down the beach towards the boat, he approached a sweater-clad figure bending over the outboard motor.

"Excuse me, Signor Alberto," he announced, tapping

him urgently on the shoulder. "I should like to take one of your crash courses in ski-ing, please. Starting now, if I may!"

The Browns gathered in a worried group on the promenade as they exchanged notes. There was so much noise going on — bursts of cheering alternating with loud groans — that it was difficult to make themselves heard; all the same it was obvious that in their search for Paddington they had drawn a blank.

"We've been to both ends of the promenade," said Jonathan.

"We've even tried the amusement arcade on the pier," added Judy. "There isn't a sign of him anywhere."

"I do hope he's not doing the undercliff walk," said Mrs Brown anxiously. "There isn't a way up for miles and he'll be most upset if he misses lunch — especially today of all days."

"Perhaps we could try asking the deck chair attendant?" suggested Judy. She pointed to a figure a little way along the front. "I bet he's good at remembering faces."

The deck chair attendant was hovering on the edge of a crowd who were leaning on the railings watching something that was taking place far out at sea, and he didn't look best pleased at being interrupted.

"A bear?" he said. "Wearing a duffle coat and carrying an umbrella. I expect that'll be the one I moved on about half an hour ago."

"You moved him on!" exclaimed Mrs Bird severely. "I'll have you know it's his birthday!"

"I daresay," said the man, wilting under her gaze, "but I never intended to move him on that far."

He pointed to a spot beyond the end of the pier, where a speedboat was bobbing up and down in the water. As the Browns turned to follow the direction of his arm there was a roar from his engine and the boat moved off. Almost immediately a small, but familiar figure rose up out of the water a little way behind. It hovered on the surface for a moment or two and then, to a groan of disappointment from the crowd, slowly disappeared into the sea again.

It was only a fleeting glimpse, but brief though it was, the Browns gasped with astonishment.

"Good gracious!" cried Mrs Bird, "What on earth's that bear doing now?"

Mrs Bird's question wasn't unreasonable in the circumstances, but it was one which even Paddington himself would have been very hard put to answer. In fact, he'd been asking himself the very same thing a number of times over the last half hour. Although he had to admit that he'd enrolled for one of Signor Alberto's special 'crash' courses, he hadn't expected there to be quite so many crashes. As far as he could make out every time he tried to do anything at all it ended in disaster.

But if Paddington was taking a gloomy view of the proceedings, Signor Alberto looked even more down in the mouth. The change in the weather had brought about a big enough drop in his takings as it was, but with what seemed like the whole of Brightsea watching his attempts to teach Paddington to water-ski he was beginning to think that trade might never pick up again. As he sat huddled in the back of the boat he looked as if he very much wished he was back on the sunny shores of his native Mediterranean again.

"Please," he called, making one last despairing effort, "we will try once more. For the very last time. Relax. You are toa da stiff. You ava to relax. You are like a stick in zee water."

Listening to Signor Alberto's instructions, Paddington suddenly realised that one of his problems was the fact that he still had Mrs Bird's umbrella under his duffle coat, so while the other's back was turned he hastily withdrew it, made some last minute adjustments to the tow rope and then lay back in the water again with the skis pointing upwards as he'd been shown.

Signor Alberto looked back over his shoulder, but if he felt any surprise at seeing Paddington's latest accessory he showed no sign. In fact he looked as if nothing would surprise him ever again.

"Now," he called. "When I open zee throttle and we begin to move, you 'ave to pull on zee rope and push with your legs into zee water. Remember, whatever you do . . . watch zee 'eels.

Paddington looked most surprised at this latest piece of advice. He'd never actually seen a real live eel before, and as the boat moved away from him and took up the slack he peered into the water with interest.

Slowly and inexorably the boat gathered speed as Signor Alberto pushed home the throttle. Suddenly the rope tightened, and for a second or two it seemed as if he was about to be cut in two. Then gradually he felt himself begin to rise out of the water.

He'd never experienced anything quite like it before, and grasping Mrs Bird's umbrella he began to wave it at Signor Alberto for all he was worth.

"Help!" he shouted. "Help! Help!"

"Bravo!" cried Signor Alberto. "Bravo!"

But there was worse to follow, for no sooner had Paddington become accustomed to one motion than there was a click and a sudden tug, and to his alarm Mrs Bird's umbrella suddenly shot open and he felt a completely new sensation as he rose higher and higher into the air.

The promenade loomed up and then disappeared as they turned at the very last moment and headed out to sea again. The cheers from the watching crowd almost drowned the noise of the engine, but Paddington hardly heard, for by that time there was only one thing uppermost

in his mind – and that was to get safely back on to dry land again.

Mrs Bird had said that he might need her umbrella in case he got taken unawares, but as far as Paddington was concerned he'd never been taken quite so unawares in the whole of his life, for as he glanced down he saw to his horror that the sea, which a moment before had been skimming past his knees, was now a very long way away indeed.

Mrs Bird opened and closed her umbrella several times. "They certainly knew how to make them in those days," she said with satisfaction.

"I bet they never thought it would be used for a bear's parachute ski-ing," said Judy.

"Perhaps Paddington could write a testimonial?" suggested Jonathan.

"I think we've had quite enough testimonials for one day," said Mrs Bird.

The Browns were enjoying a late lunch in a restaurant overlooking Signor Alberto's ski-ing school.

Paddington in particular was tucking in for all he was worth. Although he was looking none the worse for his adventure, there had been a moment when he'd thought he might never live to enjoy another meal, and he was more than making up for lost time.

He'd fully expected to be in trouble when he got back, but in the event the reverse had been true. The Browns had been so relieved to see him safe and sound they hadn't the heart to be cross, and Signor Alberto had been so pleased at the success of his lessons he'd not only refused any payment but he'd even presented him with a special certificate into the bargain. It was the first time anyone in Brightsea had seen parachute ski-ing, and if the size of the queue on the promenade was anything to go by there would be no lack of customers at his school for some time to come. Even a man who ran an umbrella shop nearby had come along to offer his congratulations. Despite the fact that the sun had come out again, he was doing a roaring trade.

"What beats me," said Mr Brown, "is how you managed to stand up on the skis at all. I didn't think you'd ever make it."

Paddington considered the matter for a moment. "I don't think I could really help myself, Mr Brown," he said truthfully.

In point of fact, he'd wrapped the rope around himself several times just to make sure, but he'd had such a lecture from Signor Alberto afterwards about the dangers of doing such a thing ever again he decided he'd better not say anything about it, and wisely the Browns didn't pursue the matter.

"Perhaps you'd like to round things off with a plate of jellied eels?" suggested Mr Brown, some while later as they took a final stroll along the promenade.

Paddington gave a shudder. What with the ice-cream, the water ski-ing, and an extra large lunch into the bargain, he decided he'd had quite enough for one day, and eels were the last thing he wanted to be reminded of.

All in all, he felt he would much rather round off his birthday treat in as quiet a way as possible.

"I think," he announced, "I'd like to sit down for a while. Perhaps we could all go to Sunny Cove Gardens. Then you can watch the gnomes while I read my birthday cards."

CHAPTER FIVE

Keeping Fit

Clenching his paw as tightly as he could possibly manage, Paddington slowly raised his right arm until it was level with his shoulder. Then he bent it at the elbow until the paw itself was only an inch or so away from the top of his head. Breathing heavily under the strain, he held the pose for several moments while he peered hopefully at his reflection in the bedroom mirror; but apart from a few slight trembles there wasn't really much to see, and as the glass began to steam up he let out his breath and relaxed again.

Mopping his brow with the end of the counterpane, he collapsed onto his bed and gazed disconsolately at a large pamphlet spread out in front of him.

It was full of brightly coloured pictures, most of which showed a day in the life of a gentleman called Grant Stalwart. Mr Stalwart, who seemed to spend most of his time dressed only in a pair of mauve tights, was shown in a variety of poses, a number of which were not unlike the one Paddington had just attempted.

However, looking at the pamphlet did nothing to dispel Paddington's feeling of gloom. In fact, the more he studied it the more downcast he became.

If the picture was anything to go by, Grant Stalwart was able to do the most extraordinary things with his muscles. Bags of cement, iron bars; nothing was too heavy for him to lift, or too strong for him to bend in two. One picture even showed him standing alongside a gaily decorated Christmas tree, surrounded by a crowd of onlookers in paper hats who watched admiringly as he cracked some after-dinner nuts for them between his biceps.

Having fur didn't exactly help matters, but looking at his own arms, Paddington had to admit that he couldn't see any muscles large enough to dent a soft-boiled egg, let alone crack walnut shells.

It was all most disappointing and after one more glance at the pamphlet he bent down and began to open a large cardboard box.

The box was labelled GRANT STALWART'S WORLD FAMOUS

HOME BODY-BUILDING OUTFIT, and on the lid was yet another picture of Mr Stalwart himself.

Paddington's interest in the subject had begun soon after his visit to the seaside. While at Brightsea he'd noticed some lifeguards doing their exercises on the beach, and at the time he'd been most impressed by the things they were able to do. Then, shortly afterwards, he'd come across an article in one of Mrs Brown's magazines about the dangers of taking oneself for granted, and his interest had been aroused again.

After reading Mrs Brown's article he'd spent several mornings doing press-ups on the bathroom floor, carefully testing himself on the scales both before and after. But either there was something very wrong with the scales at number thirty-two Windsor Gardens, or the marmalade sandwiches he'd eaten afterwards in order to restore his energy had more than made up for any lost weight, for if anything the needle had gone up slightly each day rather than down.

It was when he'd been glancing through the magazine again in the hope of seeing where he might have gone wrong that he'd come across Grant Stalwart's advertisement.

Not even his worst enemy could have accused Grant Stalwart of taking *his* body for granted, and the advertisement was ringed with pictures of cups and medals he'd won in nearly every country in the world. According to Mr Stalwart the apparatus which had turned him into such a he-man was worth at least twenty pounds of anybody's money, but notwithstanding that he seemed more than eager to share the secret of his success with anyone who cared to write in, provided they enclosed a one pound note. However, the thing which really clinched matters for Paddington was the solemn promise to any of his customers that if by the end of the first week they weren't filled to the brim with boundless energy he would refund their money without question.

There was a lot more in small print at the bottom of the advertisement, but Paddington didn't bother to read it; instead, he turned his attention to a section marked 'Testimonials from Satisfied Customers'. Although none of them seemed to be from bears it still struck him as a very good bargain indeed, and he lost no time in completing his application form and sending it in.

But far from being filled with boundless energy, Paddington felt so worn out after his exercises it was as much as he could do to read through the instructions again, let alone ask for a refund.

The apparatus consisted of two tightly-coiled springs which were attached at one end to a large metal plate. Each spring had a wooden handle at its opposite end, and the plate itself came ready-drilled with four holes and some special non-slip screws, so that it could be fixed to a convenient wall.

There were a lot of walls at number thirty-two Windsor Gardens, all of which looked only too convenient by Mr Stalwart's standards, but somehow Paddington couldn't picture the Brown family being very enthusiastic about

having any springs screwed to them.

He tried jamming the plate between the bedrails, but after pulling the bed round the room several times without the springs giving so much as a creak let alone showing any signs of expanding, he gave up in disgust and decided to try his luck in the garden.

A few moments later he hurried outside armed with Mr Brown's bag of tools and was soon hard at work screwing the plate to a part of the fence that was safely hidden from the house by the garden shed.

After testing it several times in order to make sure it was firmly fixed, Paddington consulted his instructions again.

Mr Stalwart seemed to have no trouble at all with *his* apparatus. Muscles rippling, his tanned body gleaming, he scarcely batted an eyelid as he extended the springs to almost double their normal length; but however hard Paddington tried he couldn't manage to pull his own springs apart by more than an inch or two, and when he did let go for a quick breather they shot back, catching his fur in the spirals and pinning him to the fence.

After a short rest Paddington decided to have one more go. He freed himself from the springs and then gathered some spare stones from Mr Brown's rockery and placed them in a row along the ground so that he would have a good foothold.

This time he had much more success. After he'd got beyond a certain point it became easier, and he was just glancing round to see if there were any more stones when he nearly jumped out of his skin as a loud cry rang out.

"Bear! What are you doing to my fence, bear?"

Paddington wasn't at all sure what happened next, but in his fright he let go of the springs and as he toppled over he heard a loud crash from somewhere behind him.

When he picked himself up and looked round he saw to his horror that Mr Curry was dancing up and down on the other side of the fence clutching the end of his nose.

Ever since the unfortunate episode with the vacuum cleaner Paddington had managed to avoid meeting Mr Curry. In fact, had he been asked to produce a short list of the people he least wanted to see, Mr Curry's name would have occupied the first three places.

Anxious to make amends, Paddington hurried across the garden and peered over the top of the fence at the

Browns' neighbour. "I'm sorry, Mr Curry," he exclaimed. "I didn't know you were poking your nose into my business."

Mrs Bird was always going on about Mr Curry, and the way he poked his nose into other people's affairs, but as soon as the words had left his mouth Paddington realised he had said the wrong thing.

He held up the springs. "I was only testing my new body-builder, Mr Curry," he exclaimed. "If I'd known you were there I would have waited until you had gone."

"Perhaps you would like to have a go?" he added hopefully, picking up Mr Stalwart's brochure and opening it at a page where a particularly skinny-looking man was shown struggling with a dumb-bell. "It's meant for seven-stone weaklings. There's a letter here from one just like you."

"What!" Mr Curry grew purple in the face. "Are you calling me a seven-stone weakling, bear?"

Paddington nodded, oblivious to the gathering storm clouds on Mr Curry's brow. "He's written a testimonial saying how good they are," he continued eagerly. "I expect if you had a go every day you could become an eight-stone weakling in no time at all. It's worth over twenty pounds and if it doesn't work you get your money back."

Mr Curry had been about to launch forth into a long tirade on the subject of bears in general and the one living next door to him in particular, but he suddenly seemed to change his mind.

"Twenty pounds?" he mused. "And you say there's a money-back guarantee?"

"Oh, yes, Mr Curry," said Paddington earnestly. "I wouldn't have got them otherwise."

"In that case," said Mr Curry briskly, "they certainly need a proper trial. I suggest you use the wall in my boxroom."

Paddington looked at Mr Curry rather doubtfully. "I think I would sooner use one of Mr Brown's walls, if you don't mind . . ." he began.

"Nonsense, bear!" snorted Mr Curry. And to avoid any further argument he reached over the fence in order to assist Paddington over.

"I shall test them myself," he announced grimly. "And if they don't work I shall lodge a complaint with the manufacturers. Don't you worry – I'll make sure we get our money back."

"*Our* money, Mr Curry?" repeated Paddington. "But . . ."

Mr Curry held up his hand. "Don't say another word, bear!" he exclaimed. "Fair's fair. I shall have to deduct the cost of making good the damage you did the other day in my dining-room, of course. But I see no reason why you shouldn't receive a small percentage as well . . . *if* there's any left over."

Paddington began to look more and more unhappy as he carried his belongings into the house and followed Mr Curry up the stairs leading to his boxroom.

The Browns' neighbour had a way of twisting words so

that even the most outrageous things sounded perfectly reasonable. All the same, he knew better than to argue for fear of making an already bad situation even worse, and he watched carefully while Mr Curry cleared a space and demonstrated exactly where he wanted the apparatus fixed.

"If you make a good job of it, bear," he growled, "I *may* not report our little upset just now. I shall be out for a while doing my shopping. I have to go to the chemist to get some ointment for my nose. You can have it ready for me to test when I get back."

Mr Curry took a deep breath and pounded his chest. "There's nothing like a spot of limbering up before the real thing."

Whatever else he might have said was lost in a burst of coughing, as he staggered out of the room and disappeared down the stairs. A moment later there was a loud bang from the direction of his front door and all was quiet again.

Heaving a deep sigh, Paddington turned his attention to the matter in hand. He wasn't at all keen on doing jobs for the Browns' neighbour, for they had a nasty habit of going wrong, and it was with a distinct lack of enthusiasm that he picked up Mr Brown's drill and set to work on the first hole.

Paddington had drilled holes in walls on several previous occasions and he'd always found it much harder than it looked when other people were doing it, but for once he had a pleasant surprise. Either Mr Curry's plaster was unusually soft, or Mr Brown's drill was extra sharp, for it went into the wall like a knife through butter and in no time at all he had four neat, round holes ready to take the plugs for the screws.

However, if Paddington had learnt one lesson in life it was that there is a reason for everything, and it was when he pushed a plug into the first hole that he discovered why it had been so easy. Mr Curry's boxroom wall wasn't made of brick at all, but some kind of soft plasterboard. No matter how many plugs he pushed into the hole they simply disappeared from view, falling down behind as if into some bottomless pit. Mr Brown's box of plugs was a big one, but even so it was only a matter of moments before it was completely empty.

Paddington surveyed the scene with growing dismay. After Mr Curry's dire warnings there was only one thing he could picture which would be worse than making a poor job of fixing the springs to the wall, and that was leaving four unfilled holes instead.

As a last resort he tried using some extra-long screws in the hope that they would go right through into the other side, but as he contemplated the drunken way the apparatus was hanging he had to admit at long last that he was beaten.

Paddington took another look inside the box. Considering the number of different walls Mr Stalwart seemed to use for his equipment he felt sure he must have come up against the same problem at some time in his life; and sure enough, attached to the inside of the lid was a small packet he hadn't noticed before, and which had been put there to deal with just such a situation.

When he opened the packet four screws fell out, and each had spring-loaded side pieces, especially made to pop out behind hollow walls as soon as they reached the other side.

It needed only a few seconds' work with a screw-driver and the plate was safely in place. He was only just in the nick of time, for as he was putting the finishing touches to the last screw he heard the front door bang, and Mr Curry's footsteps began to draw near.

As he entered the room he eyed Paddington's handiwork approvingly. "Very good, bear!" he exclaimed, removing his coat. "Stand well back. I'll just show you how it should be done before I get in touch with the manufacturers."

Rubbing his hands together, Mr Curry picked up the handles, closed his eyes, and gave the springs a sharp tug.

If he didn't actually look like Grant Stalwart it wasn't for want of trying. With his lips tightly compressed, he struggled to gain a foothold on the linoleum. Paddington did as he was told and stood well back, for he had no wish to be in the way if his screws did come out. But Mr Stalwart's special expanding screws were more than equal to the task. The plate was firmly fixed.

"I think, Mr Curry," he announced, "that the wall will come away before my springs do."

In the past Paddington had often noticed that many a

true word was spoken in jest, but even so he was even less prepared than Mr Curry for what happened next.

The words had hardly left his mouth when there was a splintering noise and the Browns' neighbour suddenly shot past. Taking with him a sizeable part of the wall as well, he disappeared through the open doorway like a bullet from a gun.

In the silence which followed there was a sound not unlike dried peas raining down as Mr Brown's plugs fell through the gap in the wall and rolled across the floor. But Paddington was oblivious to them. He did the only thing possible under the circumstances. Hurrying across the room he hastily locked the door before Mr Curry had time to recover. Then he sat down on his box and gloomily contemplated the hole in the wall while he waited for the storm to break.

Mr Curry held out a sheet of typewritten paper. "Sign here, bear," he growled.

Paddington looked round at the Browns for guidance and then at a nod from Mrs Bird he picked up a pen and carefully wrote down his name, adding his special paw mark for good measure in order to show that it was genuine.

"Good," said Mr Curry. "I hope this will teach you a lesson, bear."

"This piece of paper," he reminded his audience, "makes over all rights in the apparatus to me."

"That means," he continued, "that any money due

back under the guarantee will now come straight to me. I had intended," he said meaningly for the Browns' benefit, "to share the proceeds, but in the circumstances I feel quite within my rights to keep it all. Good-day!"

Mr Brown looked from one to the other as Mr Curry left the house. He'd come back from his office rather late in the proceedings and so far he had only received a garbled version of all that had taken place.

"You're not letting him get away with it, are you?" he said. "If you ask me, seeing how he more or less browbeat Paddington into lending him the springs in the first place it would serve him right if he lost the twenty pounds and had to keep them."

"Twenty pounds?" echoed Mrs Bird, with a twinkle in her eyes. "Who said anything about twenty pounds?"

Mrs Brown held up a copy of her magazine and pointed to Grant Stalwart's advertisement. "They may be worth that much," she said, "*after* they've been paid for. But I'm afraid the pound Paddington sent in was only a deposit. There are another nineteen to go."

Paddington nearly fell off his chair with surprise. "I've got another nineteen pounds to go!" he exclaimed in alarm.

"No, dear," said Mrs Brown. "*You* haven't, but Mr Curry has."

As the full meaning of the situation sank in, Mr Brown began to chuckle. Then he felt in his wallet and took out a one pound note.

"I think," he said, "that Paddington ought to have his

deposit back. It's worth every penny just to see right triumph over wrong for a change."

"Thank you very much, Mr Brown," said Paddington gratefully.

"I should be careful how you spend it this time," said Mrs Bird. "And always read the small print at the bottom of any advertisements."

Paddington locked the note away in his suitcase and then put the key inside his hat for safety. "Oh, I shall, Mrs Bird," he said earnestly.

"Perhaps," he added, as he considered the matter, "I could buy myself a magnifying glass just to make sure."

He reached out in order to help himself to some much needed toast and marmalade, and as he did so he caught sight of his reflection on the side of the tea-pot.

"And if I have any change," he added thoughtfully, "I may buy some nut-crackers. I don't think my muscles will ever be big enough to manage your Christmas walnuts."

CHAPTER SIX

Paddington in Touch

"Good heavens!" exclaimed Mr Brown, as he opened the post at breakfast one morning. "Fancy that!"

"Fancy what, Henry?" enquired Mrs Brown.

Mr Brown held up a short, hand-written note for everyone to see. "We've been invited to a rugby match," he replied.

Mr Brown's announcement had a mixed reception from the rest of the family. Mrs Brown looked as if she didn't fancy the idea at all. Jonathan and Judy, who were enjoying the first day of their Christmas holiday, obviously fell in opposing camps. Mrs Bird passed no comment, and it was left to Paddington to sway the balance.

"A rugby match!" he exclaimed excitedly. "I don't think I've ever been to one of those before, Mr Brown."

"Well, it's really through you we've been asked at all," said Mr Brown, as he re-read the note. "It's from the headmaster of your old school. It seems they're having an end-of-term game in aid of charity. It's between the sixth form and a touring side from South America – the Peruvian Reserves. I expect that's why they thought of you."

"I didn't even know they played rugby in Peru," said Mrs Brown.

"Well, there must be at least twenty-six of them," said Mr Brown, "if they've managed to send over their reserves."

"You can borrow one of my old rattles if you like," said Jonathan.

"It had better be one that works both ways," broke in Judy. "Don't forget, Paddington's loyalties are going to be divided."

Paddington jumped up from the table clutching a half-eaten slice of toast and marmalade in his paw. "My loyalties are going to be divided!" he exclaimed in alarm.

"Well," said Judy, "you won't know which side to cheer. After all, it *is* your old school, and you do come from Darkest Peru."

Paddington sat down again. "Perhaps I'd better have two rattles," he said. "Just to be on the safe side."

"Don't you think a couple of flags might be better?" said Mrs Brown nervously.

"*Small* ones," agreed Mrs Bird. "We don't want any eyes poked out in the excitement. You know what rugby crowds are like, and there's no knowing what might happen once that young bear gets worked up."

With the memory of other sporting functions Paddington had attended still clear in her mind the Browns' housekeeper was beginning to wish she'd taken a firmer stand at the start of the conversation.

But it was too late. Paddington was already helping Mr Brown compose a letter of thanks to the headmaster, and as soon as breakfast was over he made preparations to go down to the market in order to see his friend Mr Gruber.

Paddington had sometimes seen rugby being played on television, but it had always looked rather complicated and he'd lost interest after a moment or two. Going to see a real game, particularly one involving his country of birth and his old school, was quite a different matter and he decided he ought to know something more about the game. Paddington felt sure that among his many books Mr Gruber would have something on the subject, and as usual he wasn't disappointed.

After a few minutes' search his friend came up with one entitled "RUGBY — ALL YOU NEED TO KNOW FOR FOUR-PENCE", which seemed very good value indeed.

But Mr Gruber waved aside both Paddington's money and his thanks. "I've had that book for more years than I care to remember, Mr Brown," he said, "and if it helps you out then I shall be more than pleased."

As Paddington got ready to leave, Mr Gruber announced that he would be closing his shop the following afternoon so that he, too, could go and watch the match. "I'll probably see you in the stand, Mr Brown," he said.

Paddington looked rather embarrassed. "I think we shall be sitting down, Mr Gruber," he said. "Mrs Bird told me I would have to wrap up well and to take a cushion because the seats are very hard."

Mr Gruber laughed. "When you go to a rugby match, Mr Brown," he said, "they call the places where you sit 'stands'. I'm afraid it's rather like the game itself – it's a bit difficult to explain."

As he took in this piece of news Paddington felt more pleased than ever that he'd managed to get hold of a book on the subject and he hurried home to study it.

After a quick lunchtime snack he wasn't seen again for the rest of the afternoon, but if the sounds emerging from his bedroom were anything to go by it was obvious that he was getting a good deal of value out of Mr Gruber's book. Some of the bangs and thumps were very loud indeed, and they were punctuated every now and then by piercing blasts from a whistle and a noise which sounded not unlike that of crunching gears.

"Thank goodness the Peruvians haven't sent over a team of bears!" exclaimed Mrs Bird, voicing everyone's thoughts as Paddington's rattles rent the air for the umpteenth time. "If it sounds like that now, goodness only

knows what it'll be like on the day."

When Paddington eventually came downstairs again his forehead looked suspiciously damp and there were several pillow feathers sticking to his fur. He had reached a particularly interesting section of his book called TACKLES — AND HOW TO DO THEM, and for the remainder of that day the Browns gave him a wide berth, especially as he kept casting thoughtful glances at their ankles whenever they went past.

Paddington slept well that night. In fact, after all his exertions he overslept and when he eventually came down he was already dressed for the afternoon's match. Remembering Mrs Bird's warnings, he was wearing not only his duffle coat and hat, but two enormous scarves into the bargain; a blue one in honour of the Peruvian side, and a red one in the school colours.

93

Apart from that, he was also carrying a large cushion, his suitcase, two rattles, a flag, a Thermos of hot cocoa, and a pile of marmalade sandwiches – several of which he ate in order to pass the time while he was waiting to go.

Because of the importance of the occasion the school had taken over a small stadium next to their grounds, and when the Browns left the house a sizeable crowd was already beginning to make its way there.

Catching sight of some of his friends from the market Paddington began to wave his flag, and by the time they joined Mr Gruber in the stand and the moment for kick-off drew near even Mrs Brown and Mrs Bird began to be infected by the general air of excitement.

Mindful of the nearness of Paddington's rattles, Mrs Bird handed round some pieces of cotton wool for their ears, and as the two teams trotted out on to the field they all settled back to enjoy themselves.

Paddington decided to keep one rattle in his right paw for St Luke's, who were at the far end of the field, and the other one in his left paw for the visiting team.

At first there was very little to choose between the two, but gradually the amount of noise issuing from his left paw grew less and less until eventually it petered out altogether.

It was clear from the start, that, good though they were, the visiting side were no match for Paddington's old school. The sixth form towered above their opponents and no matter how hard they tried, the Peruvian forwards couldn't penetrate their defences. In fact, the only good thing about it all was that for the most part play took place at the end of the field where the Browns were sitting, so that Paddington had a good view of the game.

Despite reading Mr Gruber's book, he was hard put to follow what was going on. As far as he could make out as soon as anyone picked up the ball the referee blew the whistle and they had to put it down again, after which most of the players formed up in a circle with their heads together as if they were having some kind of discussion.

Paddington grew more and more upset as the game progressed, and when, towards the end of the first half, one of the Peruvian players was sent off the field for what seemed like no reason at all, he looked very unhappy indeed. Far from being divided, his loyalties were now almost completely on the side of the visitors.

"I'm afraid he's been sent off because he's got what they call a 'loose arm'," explained Mr Gruber, when he saw the look on Paddington's face.

Paddington gave the referee a hard stare. "I'm not surprised!" he exclaimed.

In his letter to the Browns the headmaster had said the match was to be a friendly one, but from where Paddington was sitting it looked as if the game was getting rougher with every passing moment. The way the Peruvians kept getting thrown to the ground he wouldn't have been surprised if some of them had been sent off with loose legs as well.

During the interval Mr Gruber explained that having a loose arm simply meant the player in question hadn't been holding on to the man next to him in the scrum, and that he'd been sent off because he'd been guilty of the offence more than once.

"A scrum," said Mr Gruber, "is when the players form up into a group with their arms round each other in order to restart the game. It's very important to have it properly conducted."

Mr Gruber went on to list the various reasons for stopping and starting the game, but Paddington's mind was far away; and when, just after the middle of the second half, yet another of the Peruvian players retired hurt he could scarcely contain his indignation.

Mr Brown glanced at his programme. "That's hard luck," he said. "They're only allowed two substitutes and it seems they still have several players on the injured list from their last game. That means they'll be one short for the rest of the match!"

"Crikey!" said Jonathan. They're eight points down already. They don't stand a chance."

He looked round in order to sympathise with Paddington, but to his surprise the space next to Mr Gruber was empty.

"I think young Mr Brown is taking things rather to heart," said Mr Gruber. "He's gone off somewhere."

"Oh dear," said Mrs Brown nervously. "I do hope he doesn't get lost in the crowd."

The words were hardly out of her mouth when Judy jumped up from her seat with excitement. "Look!" she cried, pointing towards the field. "There he is!"

Following the direction of her gaze, the Browns saw a familiar figure in duffle coat and hat hurrying across the pitch.

"Oh gosh!" groaned Jonathan. "Trust Paddington."

The match was being refereed by the St Luke's games-master and he'd been about to blow his whistle to restart it when something about the way the crowd was cheering made him pause. He turned and stared at the approaching figure in surprise.

"Excuse me," said Paddington, "but I've come to offer my services. I'd like to join the Peruvian Reserves, please."

The games-master looked at him uneasily. Although he hadn't actually met Paddington before, he knew all about him from the other masters.

"I'm very sorry," he said, "but I don't think I can allow that. It really has to be someone from the country concerned."

"I come from Peru," said Paddington firmly. "*Darkest* Peru. And I'm very concerned."

"It's true, sir," broke in the school captain. "I'm sure the head wouldn't mind."

The games-master ran his fingers round his collar. "It's all highly irregular," he said. "I'm really supposed to know the names of any substitutes *before* the match, but . . ." he looked round nervously as sounds of unrest came from the crowd, "it *is* in aid of charity, and . . . er . . . if no one objects . . ."

"We certainly don't," said the St Luke's captain sportingly.

"All right," said the games-master, turning to Paddington. "I'll hold up play for a moment while you get rid of your duffle coat."

"Get rid of my duffle coat!" exclaimed Paddington hotly. He gave the master a hard stare. "I'm afraid I can't do that. Mrs Bird said I had to wrap up well."

The games-master gave a sigh. He knew he was fighting a losing battle. "Perhaps," he said, as the other players gathered round, "you'd better meet the rest of your side."

"You are good at rugby, no?" asked the Peruvian captain as he shook Paddington's paw while he introduced the other members of his team.

"Well, no," agreed Paddington. "You see I haven't actually *played* before. But I've read all about it in a book Mr Gruber lent me, and I practised some tackles in my bedroom yesterday with one of my pillows."

Fortunately the visiting team's command of English wasn't quite up to Paddington's explanations, otherwise they might not have greeted the arrival of their new team-mate with quite so much enthusiasm.

In any case there was no time to dwell on the matter, for with the crowd beginning to stamp and whistle at the long delay the players quickly formed up again and waited for the referee to blow his whistle.

Paddington watched as they formed a scrum and one of the St Luke's team threw the ball into the tunnel formed by their legs.

There was a flurry of movement and almost immediately the ball came flying out again and as luck would have it landed right at his feet.

Paddington raised his hat politely to thank the player who had thrown it, and then picked the ball up in order to examine it more closely. He'd never actually seen one close to before and he hadn't expected it to be quite so oval in shape. He was just wondering if he ought to tell the referee in case it had been squashed with all the rough play, when there was a pounding of feet from somewhere behind and what seemed like a ton weight suddenly landed on top of him.

For a moment Paddington lay where he had fallen, all the breath knocked from his body, and with a hard lump in the middle of his chest which, as he came to, he gradually realised came about because he was still clutching the ball.

"Very good," said the Peruvian captain as he helped

Paddington to his feet. "We have gained two yards. Only eighty more to go. Now we have another scrum."

"*Another* one!" exclaimed Paddington in alarm. He began to move back in case the same thing happened again, but before he had time to get very far, let alone regain his second wind, the game was in full swing once more and one of the Peruvian forwards was already racing full pelt towards him.

"Catch!" he shouted, throwing the ball to Paddington.

"I don't want it, thank you very much," cried Paddington, and as the ball landed in his paws he threw it up the field as hard as he could.

Almost immediately the referee blew his whistle.

"You're not supposed to throw it forwards," he said. "You're supposed to throw it back down the field."

Paddington stared at him in astonishment. If that was the sort of rule the Peruvians were up against it was no wonder they were losing.

"Perhaps," said the captain, as the players formed up again, "you would like to be our 'hooker'?"

"That's the chap who has to try and get the ball when it's thrown into the scrum," explained one of the St Luke's side, catching sight of the puzzled look on Paddington's face.

Paddington eyed the other players doubtfully. He didn't like the way some of them were looking at him at all. All the same, he was a game bear at heart, and after a moment's hesitation he joined in the scrum and waited for the ball to arrive.

To his surprise it landed somewhere in the middle of all the legs and then bounced straight back into his paws.

Hastily putting it inside his duffle coat for safety, he broke free of the scrum and hurried off down the field as

fast as his legs would carry him. As he neared the far end he took a quick glance over his shoulder, but the rest of the players seemed to be having some sort of an argument with the referee and no one except the crowd was taking the slightest interest in his activities.

The roar which went up as Paddington placed the ball on the outer side of the touch-line completely drowned the cries from the other players when they discovered what had happened. But jumping with joy, the Peruvian side came running down the field in order to pat Paddington on the back.

"Is a very good try," said the captain. "Is a best try I never seen."

"Now," he added dramatically, "all you 'ave to do ees improve it and we are 'aving five points."

"I don't think I *could* improve it," gasped Paddington. "I don't think I could run any faster if I tried."

The games-master took a deep breath. He still couldn't understand how Paddington had managed to escape his and the other players' notice, but seeing was believing.

"He doesn't mean he wants you to do it all again," he said wearily. "He means you've scored three points for placing the ball over the line. Now, if you manage to kick the ball between the posts and over the cross bar you get two more points. That's what's known as 'improving' it."

Paddington gazed up at the goal posts while he considered the matter.

"I think I like it the way it is," he announced.

"In that case," said the captain, "I will call on Fernando."

Signalling to one of the other members of the team he stood back with the rest of the players and waited expectantly.

"Hooray!" shouted Jonathan, as there was the sound of leather hitting leather and the ball sailed between the posts. "Five points to Peru!"

"*Darkest* Peru!" added Judy.

But their voices were lost amid the renewed cheers which rose from all around at the unexpected turn of events.

"Do you think they'll do it again?" asked Judy anxiously

as the two teams ran back up the field amid a buzz of excitement.

Mr Brown glanced at his watch. "They'll have to look slippy," he said. "We're into extra time already."

Although none of the Peruvian side knew how Paddington had managed to fool their opponents, they knew better than to change their luck once it was running their way, and they made sure he was given possession of the ball as soon as it was in play.

Once again, with it safely tucked beneath his duffle coat, he hurried back down the field.

But this time the other side had him marked, and with one half of the team protesting to the referee as they realised what was happening, the rest set off in hot pursuit. Like hounds who had caught the scent of a fox, they gave chase, uttering whoops of revenge.

Paddington ran as fast as he could, but size for size his legs were no match for the sixth formers of St Luke's, and they were gaining on him rapidly.

To roars of encouragement from the crowd he reached the line barely a whisker's length ahead, and with no time to look over his shoulder let alone stop to put the ball on the ground, he tore on for all he was worth.

He was dimly aware of a figure approaching him across the turf. Whoever it was had come from the crowd behind the goal area and was waving at his pursuers. He only just managed to pull up in time before they collided. As it was, they both fell to the ground and any remarks they might have exchanged were lost for all time.

At almost the same moment a long drawn-out blast from the referee's whistle brought both the St Luke's forwards and the game to a halt.

"What rotten luck!" exclaimed Jonathan. "Fancy getting in the way just as Paddington was about to save the game!"

"Rotten luck, nothing!" said Mr Brown, waving his programme in the air. "That's one of the rules of the game. You don't have to touch the ground. You can score a try by touching a spectator or an official provided they're not more than twelve yards beyond the goal."

"That means they've drawn then!" cried Judy excitedly. "Listen to everyone cheering."

"I'm not surprised," said Mr Brown. "Whatever the rights and wrongs of the matter, I think the crowd's had its money's worth. I doubt if they'll see a better game this season."

"Hear! Hear!" agreed Mr Gruber. "And I think a draw is a very fair result in the circumstances." He broke off as he suddenly caught sight of a strange expression on Mrs Bird's face. "Is anything the matter?" he asked with concern.

"I'm not sure," said the Browns' housekeeper faintly. "I'm really not sure at all. Will someone please tell me if I'm seeing things?"

As the others turned, they too caught their breath in surprise as they saw Paddington heading in their direction accompanied by his helper from the crowd.

She wore an odd-looking bowler hat and a poncho

which was more than a little mud-stained and ruffled, but there was something very familiar about her nevertheless.

"Excuse me," said Paddington as they drew near, "but I'd like to introduce you to my Aunt Lucy!"

CHAPTER SEVEN

Comings and Goings at Number Thirty-two

To say that the Browns could have been knocked down with a feather by Aunt Lucy's unexpected appearance at the rugby match wouldn't have been too much of an exaggeration.

They had all become so accustomed to the thought of her being a part and parcel of the Home for Retired Bears in Lima that never in their wildest dreams had they pictured her ever leaving its gates, let alone visiting England.

"Mind you," said Mrs Bird, when she came downstairs the next morning carrying Aunt Lucy's breakfast tray, "the more I think about it the less surprised I am. I can see now where Paddington gets his sense of adventure from."

"Don't tell us *she* stowed away in a lifeboat too!" exclaimed Mr Brown.

"No," said Mrs Bird. "She came by air – on a package tour. She's a founder member of the Peruvian Reserves Supporters Club, and she gets special privileges."

"Does that mean she won't be staying very long?" asked Mrs Brown.

"Ah, now that I can't answer," replied the Browns' housekeeper. "And I'm not sure if we ought to mention it at this stage. It might sound rather rude."

It was obvious that as far as Mrs Bird was concerned Aunt Lucy could stay as long as she liked, and the Browns hastily changed the subject.

In any case, there were lots of things to talk about, and so many plans to be made that Jonathan, Judy and Paddington filled up several pages of an old exercise book with a list that included everything from a visit to Paddington Station to watching the Changing of the Guard.

When Aunt Lucy finally appeared she was dressed ready to go out. To the Browns' surprise she still had a label attached to her poncho. It was not unlike the one Paddington had first worn. On one side it said: PERUVIAN RESERVES SUPPORTERS CLUB, while on the other it had her name, AUNT LUCY, written in large capital letters, and her address: c/o THE HOME FOR RETIRED BEARS, LIMA, PERU.

"Never go out anywhere without a label," she said firmly, when she saw the others looking at it. "Especially in a foreign country. You never know what might happen."

"Very wise," agreed Mrs Bird. "It's a pity more people don't do it."

The next few days were hectic indeed. With Paddington and Aunt Lucy in tow, the Browns left home early each morning, seldom returning until late in the evening.

And every night, over cups of cocoa, Aunt Lucy regaled them with stories of life in Peru, and of the vast plains and mountains that lay beyond the city of Lima. At the end of it all they were usually so tired they just tumbled into bed and fell asleep as soon as their heads touched the pillows.

All in all, they weren't sorry when, a few evenings later, she announced before retiring to bed that she would like to spend a quiet time the following day doing some shopping.

Mr Brown suddenly discovered he had some urgent business to attend to at his office, and it was agreed that Mrs Brown and Mrs Bird would take the rest of the family round the shops.

For some reason best known to herself, Aunt Lucy seemed rather pleased when she heard Mr Brown wouldn't be coming with them, but it wasn't until the next day that she revealed exactly why.

"I want to buy him a Christmas present," she announced.

"Oh, you don't have to do that," began Mrs Brown.

"But I do," said Aunt Lucy firmly. "It's been a great comfort to me over the years to know that Paddington has been in safe hands and I'd like to do something in return."

"Perhaps you could get him some pipe-cleaners," said Mrs Brown vaguely. "He's always running out."

"Pipe-cleaners!" repeated Aunt Lucy, looking most upset. "I'd like something more than that."

"How about something for his boat, Mrs Brown?" suggested Paddington.

Recently Mr Brown had begun taking an interest in boats and he'd even talked about buying an inflatable dinghy large enough to take the family on summer outings. With Christmas looming up the Browns had already started buying some accessories to go with it in the hope that he wouldn't change his mind.

"We could go to the place where we bought them," said Judy.

"It's jolly good," agreed Jonathan. "They've even got a special machine where they teach you to sail. You put a coin in and it goes up and down just as if you were really at sea."

Aunt Lucy took all this information in. "I think I like the sound of that," she said, nodding her approval.

With the rest of the family wanting to do some Christmas shopping as well, it was quite late in the day before they finally reached their destination. As they entered the shop a salesman detached himself from the counter and came forward to greet them. If he was surprised by the sudden arrival of so many unseasonable visitors he managed to conceal it very well.

"And what can I do for you?" he asked, rubbing his hands together in anticipation.

"We're really looking for something suitable for an inflatable dinghy," said Mrs Brown. "It's for a small Christmas present."

The man's face fell. "Perhaps," he said, "you'd like a pump . . . or a puncture outfit?"

"A puncture outfit!" exclaimed Paddington, looking most upset. "Mr Brown hasn't even got his boat yet!"

He gazed round for Aunt Lucy to see if she had any ideas, but she was already clambering into a large boat which stood in a position of honour in the centre of the showroom.

"This is what I would like!" she said.

The salesman's face lit up. "Ah!" he exclaimed. "I can seen I'm dealing with someone who knows about these things. That, madam, is our very *best* model. It's our luxury self-inflating dinghy, as used by the navies and shipping lines all over the world." He pointed to a small canvas bag standing alongside. "You may find it hard to believe, but that's the bag it comes in. All you have to do is pull a string and in ten seconds it blows itself up, ready to use."

"It's practically unsinkable," he continued, "but should you ever find yourself in trouble everything has been thought of. It comes complete with an automatic radio distress signal, sea-sickness tablets, electric torch, fishing-line and hook, iron rations, safety-pins, and a bag of suitable sweets. It isn't simply a boat — it's a way of life!"

Paddington and Aunt Lucy exchanged glances. "It sounds very good value," said Paddington.

"I'll take one," said Aunt Lucy, opening her purse.

Mrs Brown put her hand to her mouth. "But you can't . . ." she began.

Aunt Lucy fixed her with a stare. "I've made up my mind," she said.

"It's much too expensive," warned Mrs Bird.

"I have my savings," said Aunt Lucy. "*And* Paddington's allowance."

"Paddington's allowance?" echoed the Browns.

"He's always put some money by out of his bun allowance," said Aunt Lucy. "He's often sent me a postal order, but I've never *spent* it."

The Browns looked at each other. They were learning something new with every passing moment.

"It all adds up," said Aunt Lucy. "Look after the centavos and the pounds will look after themselves," she added decidedly. "Besides it will give me a great deal of pleasure."

The Browns stood back, powerless to intervene. In any

case the salesman had already called over another assistant to help deal with his important new customer and they were both so busy washing their hands in invisible soap it was obvious there was no turning back. The Browns had no idea what the boat cost, for it didn't actually have a price written on it, and they didn't dare ask for fear of receiving another shock. But Aunt Lucy's purse was obviously more than able to withstand the strain, for the transaction was all over in a matter of seconds.

The salesman was so pleased he even let them have some free rides on the training machine, and Aunt Lucy in particular had such an enjoyable time pulling the lever which made it rock to and fro it looked at one moment as if the boat might even capsize.

But much to everyone's relief she at last consented to climb out, and with their shopping finished they made for the nearest bus stop.

The bus was crowded when it arrived, but Aunt Lucy and Paddington managed to find a vacant seat at the front of the top deck; Jonathan and Judy sat just behind them; and Mrs Brown and Mrs Bird made do with some seats near the back.

They hadn't travelled very far when Aunt Lucy suddenly looked round. "I feel sick!" she announced at the top of her voice.

"Oh dear," said Mrs Brown nervously. "Perhaps it was the boat? She did stay on rather a long time."

"And *hungry!*" added Aunt Lucy as an afterthought.

"But she can't . . ." began Mrs Brown, and then she

broke off. She'd been about to say that no one could possibly feel both things at the same time, but she changed her mind. If anything, Aunt Lucy was able to look even more determined about matters when she had a mind to than Paddington.

"Perhaps I could get some sea-sickness tablets out of Mr Brown's dinghy bag," said Paddington eagerly. "The man said there are some suitable sweets as well."

"I should get the tablets out first," called Mrs Brown. "But do it carefully," she warned. "It's so nicely packed. We don't want to get all the bits and pieces over the bus."

Paddington opened the flap of the canvas bag and felt inside. "It's all right, Mrs Brown," he called. "I think I can manage." He gave a tug at something inside. "I'll just get this piece of string out of the way first."

No one, least of all Paddington, knew quite what happened next. In any case, there was certainly no time to think about it. As he pulled the string, there was a loud hissing noise. The canvas bag started to bulge and as he staggered back clouds of material began to billow forth like some gigantic flower, growing bigger and bigger with every passing moment. The other occupants of the bus watched in silent fascination as the boat began to take shape. It filled the gangway, pressed against the roof, and overflowed onto the seats, letting nothing stand in its way.

The man in the shop had said the operation was over in ten seconds but as Paddington clambered onto his seat for safety it felt as if his whole lifetime was passing before him.

When the hissing finally came to an end, the hullabaloo

that broke out as the passengers struggled to free themselves more than made up for the silence that had gone
before.

The noise brought the conductor running up the stairs,
and when he reached the top he nearly fell backwards
down them again at the sight which met his eyes.

"'ere!" he cried. "Who brought that up?"

"I didn't *bring* it up," gasped Paddington, as he
peered over the stern. "It happened! I think I must have
pulled the wrong piece of string by mistake."

The conductor reached up and rang the bell. "Well,
you'd better pull the right one and get it off again, mate!"
he exclaimed. "Toot suite! I'm not 'aving these sort of
goings on on my bus!"

Paddington gazed at the dinghy and then at the narrow
staircase behind the conductor. "I don't think I can," he
said unhappily.

"We'll see what the Inspector 'as to say about *that*,"
said the conductor, making for the stairs. "'ere, Reg," he
called. "There's a young bear up 'ere with a boat!"

A pounding of feet heralded the arrival of the Inspector.
Taking in the situation at a glance, he removed a penknife
from an inside pocket and started to open it. "It's got a
thing-a-me-jig for getting stones out of horses' hooves,"
he said, "but I don't know about getting boats out of
buses. I'll have to use one of me blades."

Mrs Bird grasped her umbrella in no uncertain manner.
"You're not sticking any blades in that dinghy," she said
sternly. "It cost a lot of money."

The Inspector stared at her. "Are you with this bear?" he demanded.

"Yes," said Mrs Bird firmly. "I am."

"And so am I," said Mrs Brown, coming to the rescue.

"And we are too!" called out Jonathan and Judy.

The Inspector looked slightly taken aback at this rallying of forces, but before he had a chance to say anything else there was a loud groan from the front of the bus.

"Crikey!" said Jonathan. "That must be Aunt Lucy!"

"I'd forgotten about her in the excitement," broke in Judy.

The Inspector gazed in astonishment as Aunt Lucy suddenly appeared round the side of the dinghy. Her poncho was back to front; her hat was all askew; and altogether she looked very much the worse for wear.

"Are you all right, madam?" he asked, grateful for even the slightest kind of diversion he could actually understand and deal with.

"No," said Aunt Lucy sternly, "I am *not* all right. Why has the bus stopped? I want to go home!"

"She's come all the way from Peru," explained Mrs Brown, "and she's not really used to all this rushing about. I'm afraid she's feeling a trifle seedy."

The Inspector was still so taken up with Paddington and Aunt Lucy he really only half heard Mrs Brown's remark, but as he caught the tail end of it his whole attitude suddenly changed.

"Why ever didn't you say so before?" he exclaimed.

He turned to Paddington. "If you'll kindly tell me your destination, sir," he said respectfully, "I'll go down and direct the driver."

"Well, we *were* on our way to Windsor Gardens," said Paddington doubtfully. "Number thirty-two Windsor Gardens . . ."

"It's not on your route," broke in Mrs Brown.

"Think nothing of it," said the Inspector graciously. He gave the conductor a nudge. "We don't want any diplomatic incidents, do we?"

The Browns exchanged glances as he clattered back down the stairs.

"I wonder what on earth he meant by that?" exclaimed Mrs Brown.

"I don't know," said Mrs Bird. "And I certainly don't intend to ask." She cast a glance at Aunt Lucy, huddled on one of the seats with a very woebegone expression on her face indeed. "If you ask me, the sooner we get back home, the better."

The Inspector was as good as his word. Shortly after the bus started up it turned off the normal route and began threading its way through the maze of side streets leading to Windsor Gardens.

By the time they reached number thirty-two they had been joined by several more vehicles: two police cars, an ambulance, and a red tender belonging to the fire brigade.

Mr Brown was already at home, and the noise as the procession drew up outside the house brought him to the door.

"Stand back, sir," said one of the policemen as he jumped from his vehicle. "We've an emergency here. This bus has been sending out a May Day signal all the way from the West End."

"A *May Day* signal!" exclaimed Paddington in surprise as he helped Aunt Lucy down the stairs. "But it's the middle of December."

The policeman took out his notebook as a babble of voices rose from all sides.

"A May Day signal," he said severely, "is an automatic radio signal for emergencies only. It's used by ships at sea and/or aircraft when they're in distress. But I don't know as I've ever heard of it being used by a bus before."

Aunt Lucy fixed him with a hard stare. "*I'm* in distress!" she said firmly. "And I think I may have an emergency any moment now!"

The others stared after her as she hurried indoors closely followed by Paddington.

"I thought you said that bear was going to the Peruvian Embassy?" exclaimed the conductor.

"The Peruvian Embassy?" repeated Mrs Brown indignantly. "We certainly said no such thing."

"But you said she was C.D.," broke in the Inspector. "That stands for Corps Diplomatique, and people in the Diplomatic Corps are entitled to special treatment. That's why we brought her here."

"No," said Mrs Bird, as light began to dawn. "We didn't say C.D. We simply said she was feeling *seedy*. That's quite a different matter."

Mrs Brown turned to her husband. "Aunt Lucy bought you a Christmas present," she explained. "But I'm afraid it won't be a surprise any more. It's stuck on the top deck!"

The policeman snapped his notebook shut. It was becoming more and more difficult to catch up with all that had been going on, and he wasn't at all sure he wished to pursue the matter.

"I know one thing," he said. "I bet that's the only Christmas present this year that's arrived gift-wrapped in a number fifty-two London bus. Though how we're going to get it out without spoiling it is another matter."

"Perhaps," said Mrs Bird, "we could try pulling the plug out?"

"Try pulling the plug out?" repeated Mr Brown. "What is it? A bath?"

"You'll see, Henry," said Mrs Brown. "You'll see."

It was some time before order was finally restored, but when the Browns went back indoors carrying Mr Brown's boat they were pleased to find Aunt Lucy sitting at the dining-room table looking her normal self again.

Mr Brown could still hardly believe his good fortune, but she waved aside his thanks and pointed to a row of parcels neatly laid out in front of her.

"They're really meant for Christmas," she said. "But as Mr Brown's had his I thought I'd like to see the rest of you open yours before I leave."

"Before you *leave?*" exclaimed Mr Brown. "Don't say you're not stopping for Christmas Day?"

"I'm only on an excursion," said Aunt Lucy. "Besides, I always have my dinner in the Home. We have special crackers with marmalade pudding to follow."

Mrs Bird opened her mouth. She was about to say that both these items would be readily available at number thirty-two Windsor Gardens if Aunt Lucy cared to stay, but she had obviously made up her mind, so instead she joined in the general excitement as everyone began opening their parcels.

Her own present was a paw-embroidered shawl, and there was a similar one for Mrs Brown.

"What a nice thought," she said. "It will be just the thing for the long winter evenings."

Jonathan and Judy each had an enormous jar of honey. "Made," said Aunt Lucy, "by bees who live in the gardens of the Home for Retired Bears. It's very sweet because they're always getting at the marmalade."

Last, but not least, Paddington opened his parcel. It contained a wrap-round dressing-gown, and a pair of Peruvian slippers.

Everyone applauded as he put them on, and a few moments later, after Aunt Lucy had shaken hands all round, he followed her out of the room in order to test them in his bedroom.

"You don't think," said Mrs Bird thoughtfully, as their footsteps died away, "that Paddington's planning to go back to Peru with her do you?"

A sudden chill filled the air.

"It's really for him to decide," said Mrs Bird. "We can't stop him if he wants to."

"He'd have said something by now if he meant to," replied Mr Brown.

He was trying to strike a cheerful note, but he failed miserably as everyone sat lost in their own thoughts. A gloom descended on the gathering and it remained that way until a little later in the evening when the door opened again and Paddington reappeared. To their relief he was still wearing his dressing-gown.

"Isn't Aunt Lucy coming down too?" asked Mrs Brown.

Paddington shook his head. "I'm afraid she can't," he said rather sadly. "She's gone home."

"Gone home?" echoed the Browns.

"Aunt Lucy doesn't like goodbyes," explained Paddington, when he saw the look of consternation on everybody's face. "She asked me to say them for her."

He felt in his dressing-gown pocket and took out a sheet of paper. "And she gave me this for you to read."

Mr Brown took the note and held it up for all to see. It was written in large capital letters, and at the bottom there was a paw-mark to show it was genuine. It wasn't quite as neat as Paddington's, but there was an unmistakable likeness.

THANK YOU VERY MUCH FOR HAVING ME AND FOR LOOKING AFTER PADDINGTON," he read. "NOW THAT I'VE GOT USED TO IT IT DOES SEEM A FUNNY NAME FOR A RAILWAY STATION. AUNT LUCY."

Mrs Brown gave a sigh as Paddington took back the note and disappeared upstairs again. "I suppose we ought to be very thankful he isn't going," she said. "But I do wish Aunt Lucy had stopped a little longer. There are so many things I wanted to ask her. About Paddington's parents . . ."

"And his Uncle," broke in Judy. "I've often wondered what happened to him."

"And how many bears there are in the Home," added Jonathan. "And what they do all day."

"Don't you think," said Mrs Bird wisely, "that in this world it's rather nice to have *some* things left unanswered?"

"Anyway," she continued, as she stood up, "if we don't go upstairs quickly we shan't be able to say our good-nights to Paddington. After all the excitement he's had

today I should think he'll be asleep in no time at all."

But for once Mrs Bird was wrong. When they entered his room he was still very wide awake. He was sitting up in his dressing-gown, and from the bulge under his blankets it looked suspiciously as though he still had his new slippers on as well.

He was busily writing in his scrapbook. "I thought I would get everything down while I can still think of it," he said, dipping his pen absent-mindedly into a nearby jar of marmalade. "So many things happen to me I have a job to remember them all sometimes, and it wouldn't do to miss any out. Aunt Lucy always likes to hear what I've been doing."

"We thought perhaps you were going back to Peru with

her," said Mrs Brown, as she tucked him in extra tightly for the night.

"Go back to Peru!" exclaimed Paddington. He looked most upset for the moment. "I'm not old enough to *retire!* Besides, I don't think Aunt Lucy would like to think of me leaving home, even if I wanted to."

It was left to Mrs Bird to voice everyone's thoughts as they said goodnight, closed the door and crept back downstairs again.

"If anyone can think of a nicer Christmas present than that," she said, "I'd like to meet them!"